Cut Away

Cut Away

a novel

Catherine Kirkwood

ARKTOI BOOKS | *Los Angeles, CA*

Cut Away
Copyright © 2010 by Catherine Kirkwood
All rights reserved

Book layout by Sydney Nichols

Library of Congress Cataloging-in-Publication Data

Kirkwood, Catherine, 1964-
  Cut away : a novel / Catherine Kirkwood. — 1st ed.
     p. cm.
  ISBN 978-0-9800407-9-1 (alk. paper)
  1.   Women—Identity—Fiction. 2.   Surgery, Plastic—Fiction. 3.
Transgender people—Fiction. 4. Psychological fiction. I. Title.
  PS3611.I769C88 2009
  813'.6—dc22

                                        2009039758

The Annenberg Foundation, the James Irvine Foundation, the Los Angeles County Arts Commission, and the National Endowment for the Arts partially support Red Hen Press.

First Edition

Published by Arktoi Books
An Imprint of Red Hen Press
Los Angeles, CA
www.arktoibooks.com
www.redhen.org

Acknowledgements

I am profoundly indebted to my teachers: Douglas A. Martin, Alexander Chee, Bhanu Kapil, and Rachel Pollack, whose inspired insights saw this work from infancy to near completion. Thanks to the faculty, students, and staff of Goddard College, my touchstone in the persistent endeavor to keep writing at the center of life. Thank you to Red Hen Press, Arktoi Books, Tara Ison, Nickole Brown and, especially, Eloise Healy Klein for their enthusiasm, attentive counsel, and an enduring commitment to keeping literature alive with new voices.

A special thanks to Rebecca Brown, Scott Driscoll, Barbara Sjoholm, Laurie Ludwig, Michelle Munro, and the Flight Club for standing by me through the early years and feeding the flames of the smallest sparks. Also thanks to A Room of Her Own Writer's Retreats for a week in the New Mexico desert during which this work was conceived.

Deepest gratitude to my mother, father, and both of my brothers who never falter in their love, loyalty, and resilience.

Thanks also to Kayleen. Without you—my writing, my life, would be half lived.

Contents

For Mom and Dad

The cities of the interior are vast
and do not lie on any map.

—Jeanette Winterson, *The Passion*

Alexandra

The lake is a mirror with clean, pink sky inside it. I stand at the water's edge, feeling the slow tilt away from salinity reported by ecologists. It will take years, but she could recover to become that fresh, sporting jewel imagined in her heyday. It's what I love about this lake. Not the dream of what she could be or the failure of that dream but that she stretches out between the two and settles there. I lift up my arms, saluting the morning's sensuous blush.

When I turn, there is a woman watching me.

She stands by her car on the dirt in nice little Blahnik flats and fresh white linen pants. I recognize the look. It's the kind of neatly turned trick I used to try out myself, but I was too lanky and angular for it—the clothes looked like they were slipping off a bent hanger. But this woman has it just right—a slim, compact body; simple, jet black hair; nails trimmed short and done in a modest pink. It all works together. As if she's sewn right in.

I was about to go past her to the shop and shoot the breeze with Mary. She works the shop on Tuesdays. The rest of the time she runs the science lab at the local elementary school. We talk about everything: the atmosphere on the moons of Mars, how elephants scatter bones of their dead, why scientists make structures miles long to see what happens when tiny particles go very fast. All the strangest laws of the universe, it turns out, are packed inside the smallest measures. Mary, too, is more than she appears. More than the canned soup and dusty band-aid boxes she sells part time from her cousin's mini-mart. More than her plain little wooden house with green cement lawn on Biloxi road where we sit on hot afternoons and drink homemade ginger ale. She always knows something new about the world and how it fits in among the other mysteries. Nothing is ever the way you think it's going to be.

That's why I watch the woman for a moment and don't just go on past. When a stranger comes into town and stands dumb-faced at the sight of things, I wonder why. Will they stay a while or get in their car, roll up the windows, and head off to the highway? This stranger seems caught, unable to take things in or turn away. So I stop and tell her about the lake and the Colorado River breaking from its banks. She does not seem to hear me. Her skin is pearling up with heat, but she remains composed, a perfect image of herself. Her stare sees and unsees me in one go. I suspect this is her manner, but it's also something I bring out in people.

I tell her to drink water, thinking she will crack a smile and thank me. But she looks even more confused. Like a stunned bird blown off course, the native creatures bewilder her. We are getting nowhere. I smile and turn to go.

That's when she calls out, "Wait! Have you seen this girl?"

She's hooked me with a neat twist. I turn to look. Her jaw is slack, lips dry and parted. When she runs her hand across her forehead, her brow smears with the fine, blonde, lakeside dust. I remember that feeling, from when I first came to the lake, like the heat was swallowing me. She really should get somewhere cool.

It's summer; the heat will spike over one hundred by midafternoon. Stepping toward me, she holds a flyer up. For a moment, I see Olivia's face. Then the woman stumbles, falls out of her sandal, hops and winces, dangling her foot above the sand.

I don't want to bring her home. I am careful whom I invite into my life. There are steps to follow, intentions to sift, a slow, circling measure of whether things seem right. But this woman is bleeding, dehydrated, and confused. She stares at me when I offer to take her to my place. Then when I nod for her to unlock the car, she blinks and says nothing. It's unlocked so I get in. The engine's running, the air conditioning's on high, and tinted windows seal out the glare from the lake. She gets in too and pulls out of the lot. Too late, I realize I could have taken her to Mary. She works with third through six graders and is good with confused, defenseless people. Instead, I direct her through the streets, lean back into the soft, cool leather. She keeps glancing over at me, sizing me up. She opens her mouth to say something then closes it and looks back at the road. We glide along like tourists.

She waits out in the garden where there isn't any shade while I rummage through my medicine cabinet. A tube of Calendula salve. A tincture of Hypericum. I try to stay as herbal as I can, except for the hormones. The relationship I have with the squat row of plastic jars and box of glass vials is give and take. Candy-shelled goblins. I've accepted their terms. The curves of my body for my old age.

It is curious that the woman does not follow me in. It's cooler here during the mornings, sickly hot in the late afternoon. Perhaps she would be uncomfortable inside the four, plain walls. The place is small and close, but I always keep the windows clean and the light outside is bright. It does not feel closed in. The furniture is a little shabby. The worn couch has a bright Mexican throw of turquoise, yellow, and brown. Even that is looking stretched and faded. On the coffee table is a kitsch lamp from the sixties with a battered, red shade. Like the walls, the floor is also thin. Footsteps are carried throughout. Because of this, I always feel the rooms are joined together in a way they aren't in other places.

When I go back out, I take her a glass of cold water. She thanks me and drinks it down. I clean and bandage her foot. Her heels are smooth, her toenails trimmed and painted pale pink. Her trousers, rolled up to the knee, are lined in silk and have a luxurious drape. Her presence swamps the small, sun-weary courtyard.

When I send her home, I think that's all there is. I don't tell her about Olivia.

That was six months ago. A chance encounter that came to nothing. Happens all the time. But, weeks later, when a young woman's body is found that could be Olivia's, I don't think twice, I call her. That's when I get the feeling we are walking on a common floor, me in one room, Eleanor in another.

Eleanor

The images progress relentlessly, as if they are lashed to a straight, iron rod pushed from behind. In one, the girl is slight. A dark-haired ballerina in low-cut brocade and a tiara too large for her head. Her dress fans down into folds of butter cream frosting. Her torso shifts from side to side as if she is striding, but she does not move. I'm awake at three a.m. Can't get back to sleep and when I do, the girl is there again, now blonde and full breasted. She is lying on cement staring up at the sun. Her eyes are wide and dark.

In the morning, I get up, shower hot and cold, drink fresh juice then black coffee, but I feel like she's still there. Smoky blue inside my head.

In the mirror, broody half circles cradle my eyes. I step back, take in the full effect. Long, lean legs, taut torso, sinuous arms, and firm, milk-white breasts beneath sculpted collarbones. My face may look beat, but the body holds its own. Still riding hard toward that slick new prime of fifty. I leave a note for the workers to hold up until the architect comes, slip into my car, and take the canyon curves fast. At the clinic, I pull into my parking spot, duck in past the cascade of bougainvillea grown wild in the first days of summer's heat.

Sandy looks me over in one glance. Her face is wide and flat, as plain and lacking in pretension as a strip mall. A few minor fixes might lighten her up. I've suggested this before. Offered discounts. She's earned it. Office manager for fifteen years.

She nods toward the waiting room.

There are three women behind the thick plate glass: a Viking-boned blonde leafing through a magazine; an athletic thirty-something with a square, resolute face, arms folded across her chest; and a mousey little woman staring out the waiting room window.

"You got a squatter," Sandy nods toward the last. Squatters arrive without appointments and wait for an opening. I don't send them away. The waiting can be useful. They see they are not alone or, even better, run across someone they deem more desperate than themselves. When they get tired of waiting, they leave.

"Wasn't able to get much out of her."

The reception phone rings. As I walk down the hall, I hear Sandy's responses, crisp and efficient. Another cancellation. Second one this week.

On my desk is a stack of files in order of the day's appointments. I sit and sip my coffee. All returning clients. Maybe Ms. Anderson is back for the lift and Priscilla wants the rhinoplasty. They'll be surer of themselves now, more decisive. Mornings like this are pleasant, easy to keep on schedule. I buzz Sandy, tell her to send the squatter back.

A soft knock as Sandy opens the door, "Dr. Renald?" That's what she calls me in front of clients. Off stage, I'm just Eleanor.

When she leaves, the mousey woman stands in the doorway. Her hands bunch together and her eyes dart across the pale peach walls.

"Come in, please." I stand and walk toward her, hand outstretched. "I'm Eleanor."

She steps back, eyes flickering wide, then takes in the room again. "Asa."

"Sit." I gesture to the loveseat. "Please."

She hesitates, then moves to the seat and eases in. Head cocked, she examines the framed degrees. I wait, saying nothing. She must be given the chance to scrutinize. It is the only way to take back the nakedness of sitting in front of someone like me. The only way to minimize that fact that I am mentally noting her flaws, professionally assessing their magnitude, and calculating how to fix each one.

She looks from one to the next of the artful black-and-whites. Reconstructive work. Befores and afters. In one, a child's smile has been excavated from cleft palate. In another, webbed index and middle fingers have been separated, restoring function. The photos are there to reassure clients. Their own imperfections are not so remarkable, easier to talk about.

In truth, it has been years since I have performed reconstructive surgery. But they don't ever ask.

Once she gets talking, we settle on a lift and she makes a date with Sandy. All very routine. The morning slips by easily into the afternoon's appointments. I long for tomorrow—all surgery. Clients are much more interesting when they are unconscious.

"It's all right, Lisa." If she would shut her eyes and lie back I could start. She is so avian—twitchy, bead-eyed, fragile as hollow bones.

If I weren't scrubbed and gloved, I'd step out to turn up the volume on the music. Gounod's "Ave Maria." In Latin, it doesn't offend and is very calming. They come in, scan the room, take in the tray of silver instruments and bowls of white cotton wadding. They glance at the blank display on the heart monitor, the gray mask hanging from the white box, and the anesthesiologist quietly adjusting knobs. Then the music starts, voices of young boys, unwavering and pure, fill the room. They stop and just listen. The music swells, the white walls close in, and we begin.

Today, Lisa sits rigid and upright. The music is too low. Someone adjusted it without asking. I will tell Sandy to talk to staff. Leave a note for the cleaners.

She chirps, "I'm not sure. It's harder than I thought."

"Relax. Everything will be fine. Is your husband here?" I move slowly, placing my hand on her shoulder, exerting just the slightest pressure. She twitches, stays bolt upright.

"He's in the waiting room." Her eyelids flicker. She's thinking of him waiting, how he fingers the keys in his pocket when he's anxious. I nudge her gently again, and she eases down on the white padded table.

"You only need local. But you're nervous. Would you prefer more?" We've discussed all this before surgery but, in the face of it, sometimes clients change their minds.

Her consent is high-pitched and abrupt. When we're ready, I move in with the mask. In a moment, she lays loose.

As her breathing steadies, my perception hones to the details of fat depth, location of muscle insertion points, variations in the flexibility of cartilage. This moment, poised for the first cut, is my center. Without it, I would not know who I am.

I follow the curve of the crease in the eyelid with the scalpel, stretching back the excess folds of fat. The incision splits, wells with blood that I staunch with a squirt of gel. The lid shimmers, palely iridescent. I tuck the scalpel beneath, gently easing pink striations of muscle and the white corpuscles of fat from the pocket. When I parallel the first cut, a sliver of flesh slides onto the blade and lies there, a shard of white flesh against red. The remaining skin aligns perfectly. The effect will be noticeable, but its origin invisible, as if this was the way she was born.

These hours absorb me. Sustain me. Outside this room, the world mutters in some far away language I don't need to understand.

At the end of the day, I ache. It comes in a rush up through my lower back, like a vise released. I slip out of my scrubs and grab the almost-empty bottle of ibuprofen from the supply cabinet. I take four. Out front Sandy is locking up. I shake the bottle.

"Just bought that."

"I'm not sleeping well. The house is still a mess." I stay away, wait to go home until the workers are gone.

"I thought they were supposed to be done last month." Sandy brushes back her thin hair and studies me, eyes pinching. "Not again."

I don't want a lecture. I put the bottle on her desk and turn to go.

"You changed the plan again." She watches me but her hands are still moving, stacking files, tucking the phone back to the edge of the desk, making a clean space for the morning.

"The windows weren't right. It put the whole room off."

"They must think you're nuts. And made of money." She tuts, looks away. "You're not, you know."

"It needed to be re-thought."

"Same architect?" When I don't answer, "That's the third, now."

She sighs. "The repairman said those strange squeaks are the air conditioning. On the blink. The clinic needs work. You might think about scaling back the Winchester house." She stands now, thrusting her ample body against the desk.

"You're not my accountant, Sandy."

"More's the pity."

She smiles, but not in a way that softens the blow. She is not one for empathy. Sandy believes that friendship rests on the willingness to face hard facts head on. It's taken some years, but I've grown to see her lack of mercy as affection.

Outside, the evening is just coming on. A mild, hazy blue rises out of an early summer gold. On the windshield of my car, on every windshield in the small, shared lot, is a bright green flyer. Sandy usually chases off anyone who tries to advertise here. But today was busy. Must have slipped in under her radar.

I tug the paper from the wiper and am about to wad it in my fist when I see a face I recognize. A girl who stopped in a while back. Says on the flyer Missing. Last seen: The Salton Sea.

I sit in my car and read it over. Been gone six months. Since about the time I saw her.

The day started off all wrong. When I got to the clinic, a battered, putty-colored Pinto was in my spot. I found a place on the street and pumped the meter with quarters. I hate to park the Mercedes on the street. Really hate it. The car is the only place since Clarissa left where I don't feel like a balloon bumping against walls. I bought it new. Before I knew there would be a settlement or that it could be disastrous.

I have to dash through the lot for the covered patio through a winter torrent, but I stop and look back at the car in my spot. The Pinto's smashed back fender is hanging loose. A cartoon eye stares out from a crumpled bumper sticker. Something hairy and yellowy white is crushed against the window—a woman's wig, tangled and dirty. The seat is piled high with clothes.

My first appointment is with a young woman, too young, I wager. Says her name's Olivia, then shortens it to Livvy. She has extraordinary eyes, gray-green speckled with a yellowish brown. Her face is slightly unbalanced, but there is beauty, even in the disproportion. With her smooth, lanky hair, high cheekbones and deep-set eyes, asymmetry gives her face depth.

She sits in my office, arms hugging her middle, wearing a faded red sweatshirt with a tear along the shoulder seam. Her canvas tennis shoes turn inward on the carpet and her knees drop together to make an upside down V.

"I don't think I should have come," she says, rubs her palms once over her knees, and then torques her body sideways, jamming her hips back into the seat.

She tells me she got my name from a friend's mom.

"She's happy?" I ask.

"Can't shut up about it." She rolls her eyes, looks to see if I am pleased.

"You told her you wanted to see me?"

She shakes her head. "She's old. Loves hanging out with teenagers, like she's one of us. She's not. Me coming here? She'd go nuts." The girl is very young. I almost say so, but hang back. I wonder if the client we are talking about is really her mother. Then she confesses. "Thing is, it is kind of weird, even to me."

"Go on. I don't think you'll shock me." This usually does the trick. Clients imagine all kinds of strange pleas if you suggest they should; ones that make their own requests seem tame. I can see her thinking, brow-furrowed. I suspect she is worried about something I can't see. Maybe an inverted nipple. A regretted tattoo. It will likely be the smallest thing. On one so fresh, so nearly perfect, the slightest imperfection can stir the deepest uncertainties.

She picks up my portfolio and thumbs through it.

"My face. It isn't right." She closes the book, turns to gaze out the window.

Even her profile is lovely. Except maybe around the septum. Perhaps a nudge there. But in a year or two she could grow into it. She's too young for me to tell for sure, too young to even guess.

I smile reassuringly, "I don't often say so, but I see a lot of faces and yours is quite remarkable."

"It's not about being more pretty." She fiddles with the edge of her sweatshirt's sleeve. Little pieces of red thread drift down to the white, jacquard upholstery. She is quite unique, almost stunning. I wonder if she has confided in anyone: her parents, a boyfriend, a girlfriend.

"I don't understand," I tell her. She's simmering, ready to confide. All I need to do is wait. I glance at the clock. It's getting close to my next appointment.

"It's like it's not me."

I tell myself we're in known territory. When people look in the mirror and see who they believe they are, it is a powerful thing. A scalpel in skilled hands can change lives. So many women are ashamed to ask for what they want. They think they're being weak, bowing to vanity. They have to have lived a while to break through, take charge. Often girls like this end up in the office of some hack who'll do anything for a price. Gives the profession a bad name. We all end up humiliated.

I tell myself we are on track now, what she needs, the professional delicacy that will be required. I have been here before. She's still turned toward the window, as if I'm not the one she's talking to. "You understand?" she asks. "It's not me."

"I can't be like this anymore. I can't." Her jaw clenches. Not in anger, in steeled resolve. She is stronger than she looks, this one.

"Pretty's the problem. It's too much." She moves one hand over her face like she's erasing it. The other keeps working at her sleeve, fingers moving like they are figuring, tallying up as the cloth unravels.

"Pretty's the problem . . . You want less?"

I am used to the relief of confession. The thrill of decisiveness. Shame is part of the territory. But the desire to diminish, the request to be helped down a step or two in order to see oneself face to face. This is something new.

She looks at me eagerly, searching, perhaps thinking I understand. To be honest, I do not, but that she thinks so is a start.

I keep heading down the track I know. Simple forward momentum often sets things in place. I offer to do some computer imaging. Not because I intend to do the surgery.

Maybe if she sees her face on screen, she'll think twice and reconsider. I buzz Sandy. No appointments open for weeks. Then, before I can think what else to offer, Livvy is standing, her face fallen, brow heavy and flat, "I can't. It has to be soon. I'm headed out, leaving town."

"When you get back, then."

"I don't know." She inches sideways, toward the door. "I shouldn't have come." Her dingy jeans hang shapelessly from her slim hips. It is an odd feeling, watching her turn, a slippery fish.

Most clients want confidence, certainty, a strong hand. That's what I do. This one is young though. Emerging. Exposed. She does not yet know her own strength. At least not well enough to willingly give way. To lay such fierce vulnerability beneath my scalpel, it stops me short.

Suddenly I realize it's her car that's parked in my space. A vagrant's car, someone living out of it.

When I say, "Wait," she glances over her shoulder, not at me.

Then she is gone, the door to the hallway open.

I could have handled things differently. She came here for help. To me. I am used to that. Why did I blunder? I put my head down in my hands, try to play it out differently. I can't. It keeps ending before I have the chance to make it come out right.

At the patio's edge, sand-colored slate gives way to dirt, a few feathery grasses, and scrubby chaparral. Two green eyes gaze boldly from pointy wheaten fur. Loose dog? Doesn't look familiar. Then I see the gaunt torso, long legs, and wary stance. Coyote.

I sip my wine. The workers are finishing up, trying to stay quiet while they sweep out the day's mess.

It's been a long time since a coyote ventured in so close. I sometimes hear them late at night, their babies peeling off strange yips, spiraling upward toward a weird dog-based harmony. Strange togetherness they have. It's hard not to imagine their tight faces lifted to the slim wild that splits open with dark. Silent paws pacing the boundary of a shrinking territory.

This one looks wearied, hungry, and bold with it. It will get him shot. Or poisoned. Coyotes are no friend to the owners of cats and small dogs. I move slowly and sit at the pool's rim. He steps back, one paw hung, but does not turn. His eyes a feverish jade, like nightfall suspended by city lights. He regards me cautiously. For a moment, the simplicity of his brief and feral life fills me. Everything falls away: the girl, the remodel, Clarissa, and I am just an imprint on pale green eyes.

Inside the house, a door slams. The coyote turns, leaps over a shrub, darts right, and bounds away through the hillside brush.

I light a cigarette. Just one cigarette, just tonight. Time to break the rotten connections. It was Clarissa's habit. Why are those the ones that are so hard to break? How had this happened? The company of this question is getting old, but I take another long drag and invite it in. It's been almost a year since she walked out. The attorneys still haggle, hers arguing she's entitled to half, mine that we were two independent women making our own ways in the world. She's supposed to sign the settlement papers this week. We've been there before. Seems longer than the twelve years we were together.

She was nothing special at first, just a friend's girlfriend. We took up with each other casually. Transitionally. Nothing new in that. So much was going on for me: the interview in *Cosmo*, election year, my mother's diagnosis, torrential rains that gouged the coast highway. Clarissa was hardly a blip on my screen when it started. But then it went on, wildly distracting, surely temporary. A year passed. Mom died. The weather dried up. Clarissa was still there, a fact. Something I'd come to count on.

I suck sharply on the smoke. Heaven. It's been a week since I've let myself.

The problem is not that I loved and lost, although that's part of it. It's like remembering my old passion for strange cities. They were places that existed, and existed in imagination. Two places at once. Names to love: The Grand Bazaar, The Bosphorus, Haghia Sophia. The sounds indigo, thick as musk. Clarissa became like one of these words, a name for something that existed inside at the same time it existed somewhere out there, beyond where you could get to. But when? When had things like the Gate of the Dead, the sound of Clarissa bathing, the Gate of Felicity, and the smell of her sleeping exhale, become a new city?

Tired, triumphant voices echo out from the back of the house as the contractors clear out.

"Hey!" I stub the cigarette out and call through the house, "There's a cold one in the fridge for everyone!" Why not? I could use a little company. I get up, go inside, and call out the invitation again.

They respond in chorus:

"Sorry, gotta go."

"Can't. Take a rain-check, though."

"Great!"

It's the small one who is willing. She is fair and solid, all lean and taut beneath wispy bangs. I smile as I peer into the work zone. They have finished framing the last wall. It's all there now, the shape of the new room.

I make her wear her tool belt, though I can tell by the smirk as she slips it over her naked hips she's humoring me. So what? I ride that lithe, scrambling body and do not bother to make her come. She could. She is ready. Shy and eager. The sardonic attitude all bluff.

Afterwards, we have gin and tonics. No craving for a second smoke. When the girl leaves, the sky is still muddy with dusk.

On Sundays the house is quiet, clean, almost whole again. A day for lounging by the pool, reading a book. Time to sit back and enjoy the place. Most of it is just right. Small alterations on classic bones—a dash of steel in the kitchen, simplified lines in woodwork, recessed lighting on classic reproductions, and bold modern abstracts. There is a flow to the interior. One weight-bearing wall had to be removed but the others were simple. Each room progresses naturally into the next with neutral, organic colors to allow the eye to be drawn through the rooms and rest on the view.

It's just this last addition that's the problem. It's too large, or too open. The roof reaches out and up and windows flank the walls, floor to ceiling. Beyond is a stripped timber, grape hung arbor, a patio of Carrera marble, hills rolling toward the sea. It should be lovely. The final touch to the home I've always envisioned. But somehow, with the new room, the whole place falls short.

I've had the windows narrowed, the angle of the roof altered, tried different styles of casings and moldings. But it always seems a little off. It's the butt of neighborhood jokes. Not because anyone else sees its faults, but because they don't, and can't imagine why I do. My private nemesis.

I'll get out, go for a drive. The house will waste me if I don't.

I still have the flyer about the runaway girl. I think about her battered Pinto. The clothes piled up. There's nowhere I need to be. So I head out, down along the coast and then inland toward downtown, the way she must have gone. Where is the Salton Sea? Southeast. Somewhere before the border.

I cross to the eastside where the ten-lane highway is scored and patched with scraggly lines of black tar. Above, cement overpasses flash by. Mile after mile of dun stucco houses. Cheap roadside motels and mini-marts pop up to mark what used to be towns now swallowed by sprawl. So many names, I lose track. Pomona. Ontario. West Covina. After a while, I let it all blur.

Within an hour, I start wishing I'd grabbed something to eat before I left. The houses taper off. The mini-marts get more squat and dingy. There are short stretches of nothing at all. Just plain ugly dirt and scrubby weeds at the road's edge. I keep driving until I'm almost to Palm Springs. Why not zip off for a late breakfast at Angelina's? Blood orange mimosas. Goat cheese frittata. Exquisite.

My body, easy in the desert air. Clarissa's thigh still hot from morning sun.

Palm trees start to flank the road. First just a few, and then our old exit: a gentle bend between two tall, even rows of them. Those trees are really something. Tall and slim and sure. Fronds lifting indolently on the breeze. You could just lean up against them.

I drive right past, but I know the exit by heart. The road leads into the town, past green lawns and orange trees fruiting year round, right up to the condo that opens out onto the third tee. The condo she had her lawyer draw up as hers in the settlement. The same lawyer that convinced her there should be a settlement, citing recent precedents for same-sex couples that made the phrase sound solid, a stepping stone in the progression of justice.

I probably would have given it to her if she had asked. But she didn't. Went straight to attorneys like I was going to screw her. That hurt almost more than her leaving. Would I have offered up the condo? I keep trying to figure out, would I have been kinder, more generous, if I'd been given the chance? Takes me nowhere. Like I'm making things up, changing how things were. Tearing up the path to who I am now.

On the map, the highway goes across the border to Arizona, right off the end of the page. Just after Palm Springs, it cuts across the north end of the Salton Sea. A lake bigger than

Palm Springs, Palm Desert, and everything in between. All the times we came out this way, why didn't I notice before?

I can see why the girl headed for it. Must be nice. A big blue plunge of cold water in the middle of the desert. Something to see.

I drive on until I come to a peeling, parched blue billboard with a splotch of yellow sun. Cartoons of canopied fishing boats float on a perfectly round lake. Grinning fish arch above rings made from mirrored sequins shimmering brightly in the day's fierce light. Pale orange letters spell out: Welcome to Salton City Beach.

No houses flank the road from the highway. Blocks and blocks of bare, silent streets demarcate stony fields of weeds and, here and there, a concrete slab. At each intersection, road signs name the long, lonely lines of cracked pavement: "Nile," "Biloxi," "Mediterranean," and "Riviera."

The first dwelling is a double-wide split raggedly down its spine. Through the three-foot crack, I see a low table and two upholstered chairs.

The next house is buried: concrete lawn ornaments, faded pink gnomes, eyeless nymphs, and a Virgin Mary with the birds chipped off. Yellow lawn furniture is piled in haphazard heaps. The carport is jammed floor to ceiling with old avocado-colored appliances and oily automotive parts.

It goes on and on. Each house like the one on the block where the crazy person lives. They're all that way. Like one day the crazies got lifted up on a high tide and deposited here.

A girl on a bike with a low rear tire labors up the street. Her hands clench the handlebars and her calves push hard against the pedals. Pink and white plastic tassels hang from her fists.

I roll my window down and am about to call out when the air moves in. The heat and stink is like a wall—sulfur, rotted kelp, saline, the reek of still water. I stop breathing, but still gag on the stench.

As the girl comes even with the car, I lean from the window. "Have you seen this person?" I hold the flyer up for her. I feel a little crazy. What will I do if she says yes? What will I do if I find her? All this bargaining and bother from a lead six months old? I should not have come.

The girl eyes the car dumbly and then stares at the flyer. In the distance, an expanse of water lays belly up, bloated against the sky.

"Some." Her white-sandaled foot comes down off her pedal and rests on the pavement. She is wearing yellow shorts and a white T-shirt with pink flowers. Gray stains streak down the front. "Only in pictures down at the store, though. Not for real."

"Thanks, hon." My words slip out the window and shrivel with heat before they reach her. "Thank you," I throw out loudly.

She watches me as I shift into drive. Then she begins to wave urgently, gesturing upwards. I roll the window down again.

"Can you?" Her face turns up toward the sun. "Can you help me get those down? Please?" She points up. Her thin arm tapers to the fingertip. From the phone wires a pair of shoes dangle from long laces, white sneakers with black and orange soles.

"Did you lose those?" I smile now. "They look pretty big for a girl your size."

"They're my uncle Jack's. He says if I can get 'em he'll give me a dollar for ice cream."

Her hope is painful as if she knows pleading won't work, but there's no other way.

"You'll need a big ladder. I'm afraid it's not something I can help with." A cruel trick. She'd never fetch those shoes. And a dollar won't buy ice cream.

The girl nods again, this time curtly, and only once. She turns her bike around awkwardly, half on, half off, then steadies herself and pushes from the pavement.

There's something fragile and awful in the sight of her small frame teetering on the bike. "Wait!" I call out. "Come back."

She stops and turns but does not push back up the hill.

"We can give it a try." Before I know it, I'm out in the heat with her. It's suffocating. I don't know why she doesn't get sucked right up into it. She's so little, almost nothing. I kick off my shoes and step up on the leather seat and then onto the hot hood of the car. I stretch, but the sneakers are still yards beyond my reach. The soles of my feet burn. I jump down and smile sheepishly. The girl just watches, eyes wide, mouth dropping as I reach inside my purse to hand her a five dollar bill. "Tell your uncle he can get his own shoes."

She blinks and stuffs the bill in her sock, then flashes me the best smile I have seen in years. It is sweet and bright. She inhales a word of thanks and pedals off.

I roll the window up and turn the temperature as low as it will go. My body is covered in a thin film of sweat. I watch the girl pick up speed, sail over the wide open pavement, look over her shoulder, and lean into a perfectly arced left-hand turn. Then she is gone.

My feet sting as I slip them back inside my sandals. I head down to the shore. The moment I step from the car, sweat begins to collect, soaking into the lining of my bra. The beach, the parking lot gravel and dunes beyond are variations of grey-white. There is no sound. No color except the blue above and its ashen reflection. The heat makes everything withdraw.

Up closer, I see that the sand is not sand at all but broken shells and bits of fish bones. Along the water's edge are clumps of dingy yellow froth. The water is the color of beer.

Why would a teenage girl want to leave the city and come here? Was she alone? I can't help feeling I'm the one who put her here, that she's still running from me or something I'm part of. Was she coming with, or to, someone? She's strong, but could she make it on her own?

Footsteps on gravel break the silence. A tan woman in dark glasses, a gauzy peasant shirt, tapering jeans, and low black boots raises her arm high in greeting. When she passes, she nods and says, "'lo."

I start to greet her, but she keeps on walking, not looking back. She stops at the water's murky edge, lifts her two broad hands toward the sky, and turns her face up to the sun. Then her long arms come down, slowly. She turns back, smiling wide and sad.

"It's not a mistake," her voice like bourbon.

"Pardon?" The sun is bright on her dark lenses. I cannot see her eyes.

"The Sea. It's not here because of a mistake."

"I'm sorry? I don't . . ."

"When they re-routed the Colorado, it ran its banks and spilled into the basin. That's the story, anyway." She stands now, one hand on her hip, the other raised to her brow. She is tall and sturdy. Her face, square and bold, is framed in auburn haze. On her hand, three thick rings of silver and turquoise. "The lake was here long before that. Here and gone, here and gone. It's a cycle. Man thinks he creates everything. But the lake was here before they moved the river."

When I don't respond, she tilts her head, smiles tersely. Then she's off again, moving past me with steely poise, throwing advice like salt over her shoulder, "If you're out here long, drink water."

I watch her walk away. On the blistering asphalt the heels of her boots disappear in quicksilver. Then I remember.

"Wait!" I reach into my car to find the flyer. "Have you seen this girl?"

She stops and turns. I imagine her examining me beneath those dark lenses. Then she saunters back. Everything is measured and slow. She takes the flyer and examines it. When she looks up, I see her eyes. They keep moving like she's reading the air.

She makes a little sound in her throat before she speaks, "They've been looking out here for a couple months. Haven't turned up anything." She glances discretely along the cut of my blouse, my trousers, shoes, and then along the lines of my car. She shrugs and hands the flyer back.

I move to step away and my foot slides from my sandal. I teeter and then come down hard on something sharp.

She reaches, steadies me.

I curse. Whatever it is, it's still in me. A shard of metal or glass.

"Sit. Let's have a look." I feel a fool hopping at her side, but the pain is real. The car is open, and I plop down on the seat. She kneels and wraps one large, square hand around my ankle.

Her gaze levels, and she says, "Breathe in," her hand cool and dry, her grip firm. I pull away, just a little. She holds tight and yanks. My foot begins to throb.

"Bone." She holds a bloody white splinter up to the light. "Looks like a vertebrae. Fish probably." She bends to see the wound.

"Not bad. Calendula and Ledum would help."

I nod, not knowing what to say. I don't have those kinds of things on hand, even at home.

"I live just up the street," she walks around to the other side of the car. I stand to show her that I'm fine, thinking she will appreciate the excuse to leave, but she climbs in. "Come on. I'll fix you up." It's strange slipping in beside her, but also oddly okay.

We drive down a dirt road along the shore. Her place is a single-wide that's seen better days. Out back is a patio and a small, modular sunroom. Sunflowers in pots surround a garden of groomed white sand and cacti. I sit on a metal chair with torn woven backing. When she comes out, she hands me a glass of ice water. The other hand cradles two small brown bottles and a wad of cotton balls.

"I'm Eleanor," I offer.

"Alexandra," she grips my hand, still cool from the glass, squeezes lightly, and lets go. She moves away gracefully, her wrist grazing against her hip.

I have done my share of tracheal and brow bone shaves, buttocks and breast implants, and abdominal liposuction, tricks of the trade to sculpt a female body from one born male. Often the work is extreme, making the male body into one that is aggressively sexual in its femininity. Alexandra, with her herbal tinctures and four little walls poking up out of the hot, scabby dirt, does not seem any part of that.

She dabs a cotton ball with one of the bottles and then pats the middle of her thigh for me to rest my foot. I close my eyes and feel her trace the cotton over my skin. The wound stings at the edges, numb at its center. Her jeans are thin, not denim. I feel the ropey muscle of her leg bunch and relax as she bends over my foot from her short, wooden stool. The motion of her fingers around and over the cut is slow but not tentative. I let my head drop back.

I have touched the shapes of faces, torsos, calves, and felt what they will become. There is always humming beneath the skin. I feel it in the tips of my fingers. A heat rises from inside, washing over the shape that wants to be left behind. Alexandra's touch is cool. There is no welling up. No containment of something that wants out. She keeps running the cotton over the cut. Pausing. Then continuing anew. I want to tell her to stop. Enough. I don't.

She sets my foot down.

"There now." She nods, her smile no longer sad.

I watch her for a moment. She looks back quietly. There is something noble in her face. It could be enhanced, feminized, by a little rounding of the cheek and reshaping of the hairline. Softening without losing strength. I could lift the outer lids of her eyes where they turn down slightly, make them less weighted, more refined, olive-shaped. I could make her powerfully handsome, in a female way. Bring out that disturbing sensuality of gender that is slightly ambiguous, but move her more toward being seen without question as female. The male that once was would be a sensual spark, one she would smolder with.

I thank her and tell her that if there's anything I can ever do if she's ever in the city. It feels stiff and formal, but I give her my card. It's what I always do. An old habit from building up the practice.

She reads it, eyes me, and then shakes her head and laughs.

Back home, I pour myself a glass of wine and walk through the house. I take my time, noticing how it all works, how it all flows. Until I get to the new room. But I still can't see why. The drywall is in. The windows are framed. Maybe if the walls are done the color of Italian sun. Or just a simple white. I am still waiting for everything to fall into place—the color, placement and style of furniture, artwork I have noticed in galleries. All of it should condense into one solid thing.

Something is wrong. There is a pause when I look from inside to out, like tripping over a crack. I have managed to smooth out transitions everywhere else in the house. Here, even with the French doors thrown open, the outside will not come in. This room holds its own in a way I cannot get around.

It's worse when it's just me at home alone. When the workers are here, I feel like things are moving forward. But then they go, and I am stuck again. Especially tonight. After that horrible place. Knowing the girl was there and isn't anymore.

I keep thinking of her on a barren rise of sand. Nights under a cold, black sky. Days parched and raw with heat. No place to go that separates the two.

I call the police to tell them that I saw the girl in January. They come out, take a statement. Months old, it's not much of a lead. Turns out she camped alone by the lake for a week or so and then took off. Didn't tell anyone where.

Weeks pass and the renovation progresses, but not in a way that pleases me. Despite the compliments of contractors and the obvious pleasure of the architect, who has asked to photograph the job for her portfolio, I feel as if we have made a wrong turn.

But I can't figure out how to fix it. The dissatisfaction spills over into work. I see clients like caricatures of shame, sorrow, disillusion. The past courses through them like rough current. Sometimes they come too late, patterns wired hard inside musculature. Habit will drag them back.

Everywhere things that were once a matter of course have begun to seem not. Cases I would have breezed though at initial consultation get muddied. I keep wondering what I'm fixing. Even surgery is no longer as pleasurable. I keep thinking about the bits I throw away. Wondering whether they're part of something more, a thing I'm meddling with.

One morning I wake after a good sleep. No lucid dreams. No waking in the night.

Surgery starts with a new client, the mousey one who came for a consult a few weeks back. Asa is hungry for change. So eager, her skin is alive with heat.

Marking her face before surgery is not necessary. My hands have performed this kind of work many times. But I will document this one. Revive the portfolio. A fresh face. A new start.

The pen rolls smoothly beneath the rise of her cheek. She soaks this up like everything else. Her eyes are closed. Not in that tense, jittery way so typical of clients at their first surgery. Her face is relaxed, open, angelic. When she smiles, it is the smallest ripple.

I will begin with an incision above the temple, deep in the hairline. Once the muscles are tightened, the excess folds of skin can be cut away. I draw a line beneath her chin where the skin sags to highlight what will be accomplished.

The auto focus locks red. Before releasing the shutter, I notice again that vague smile on her lips. The lines above predict lean, crescent-shaped cheeks and a flare at the edge of the eyes. Shapes of youth, vigor, energy. She will look in the mirror and feel better about a lot of things. It is right that she smiles. I press the button and the flash thrusts into the space between us.

Her eyes fly open, wide and staring. The pupils, contracted by the light, are tiny and remote, as if the inside of her has fallen away. Then she blinks and adjusts.

She says, "I can feel it already."

"Yes?" I am beguiled. She is so full of hope.

"You must feel like a million bucks at the end of every day." Her voice hums like water to a tap.

I laugh, "Sometimes only a couple grand." I step toward her with the mask.

"What you do for people?" Her small eyes tuck back into her round, freckled face as she closes them. Her hair is short, red-brown, and wiry. She could be puckishly cute. But there is something calcified in the shape of her jaw and the rise of her cheek. A rigidity that softens as she goes under.

When she is out, she keeps on smiling that loose, secret smile. I can't shake the look of her. It is surprising, enchanting, to be reminded how much progress can be made even before the procedure begins.

I do not make the deep openings from which pain or death is meant to be extracted. I have always stayed outside the cage a human body is packed in. But in strange, rare moments like this, I feel in awe of the thing inside I am setting free. It has been a long time. To catch sight again of this sensibility excites me. I like working with Asa.

Her eyes will be a challenge. Both upper and lower lid require shaping. The result is as much affected by the amount and elasticity of skin as the structure of the spenoid and fissures of the skull. Not an uncommon procedure, but tricky. I feel strangely nervous.

I move faster than I should. My mind is not yet fixed on the outcome, and my hands are impatient. My thoughts try to keep up. When I touch the scalpel to her lid, it is too soon. No matter. Keep moving. My hands know the way.

The knife follows the line and the skin tips its smooth, scarlet edge outward.

I look down into the opening.

The patient's eye twitches. The hole pulls tight then slack. My hand jitters. The knife skips.

A jagged, red grin.

The next week Asa arrives angry and unannounced, scaring my clients. I have to talk her around. A skill I've honed from negotiating with Clarissa. It goes okay, but still, at the end of the day, I am glad for neat bourbon and a smoke. Sandy worked Asa in for surgery on Thursday, between two routine procedures where I can make up time. It will all be fine. I can still set things back on course. I am grateful that she did not take her complaint to my colleagues or, worse, start the expensive and mutually unsatisfying process of having her lawyer call mine. It seems like a small thing, but I am grateful to her for giving me another chance.

When Thursday passes without flaw, I think that I should celebrate. Maybe that new little French place up the coast. Hugely popular, booked up weeks ahead, but today I feel lucky. Primed to snatch up someone's last minute cancellation, I reach for my cell. A missed call is logged with no message. Perfect, maybe someone I can invite along. Can't think who it could be. When Clarissa left, even my friends drifted out of touch. The number's long distance. I don't recognize the area code. This is a private line and I take pains to keep it that way. I hit call sender.

"Eleanor? It's Alexandra. We met a few weeks ago, at the Salton Sea?"

Even as she said her name, I knew. I knew who she was by the sound she made before she spoke. A tiny little swallow. The familiarity warms me. Why? I haven't spoken to her for weeks. I hardly know her at all.

"I'm so sorry to bother you. But you were looking for a young woman, Olivia?"

"Just a minute." I dodge around a slow car ahead. "Go on."

"Maybe it's nothing. But I just thought you might want to know."

"Is she okay?"

"They found a young woman's body."

I wait. And then I ask, "It's her?"

"They don't know. Just found it. The body's wrapped in a tent flysheet."

"Jesus."

"I thought you'd want to know, that maybe you'd want to be here."

"It could be anyone." I say it, but it sounds wrong. I accelerate and shoot through the last of a yellow light.

"They're still trying to confirm identity. Maybe you should come down."

Why did the girl go to the desert in the first place? Why go at all, and why there? I thought I'd banished these questions. No matter what I do, the day she came to my office keeps shaping all that came after. I know the history of now goes way back, but in my head I keep looking for her, for some trace of where she went. Like that will tell me something. Like I'll be able to figure out whether or not I could have made a difference.

I pull across three lanes of traffic and make a U-turn, heading back to the freeway going east. Someone honks. The hell with you, I want to say. To hell with you. It's going to be a long night. I drive back up Santa Monica Boulevard, all the while thinking I'll reconsider in a moment and go to dinner, but I don't. Almost the whole drive, for more than three hours, I'm on the verge of turning back.

It's dark when I arrive. Alexandra stands on the unlit porch of the lakeside store. "It's not her," she says. "I'm sorry I called. They just notified the family and released the name. It's some other girl. Not her."

The headlights of a car blind me. Alexandra puts a long, strong arm on my shoulder and pulls me from the glare. She stands over me. The sharp tang of her. The smell of night air and sage. Knowing that it isn't Olivia out there on the spot-lit shore, I lean in, too exhausted to speak. We stand for a few minutes looking out at the vaporous glow of the lake's surface. Then she says she has a spare couch if I want to wait until morning to drive back. I hesitate. I can get a nice room in Palm Springs. I know plenty of places that would give me their best. She's got her hand on my shoulder, something most people won't dare do. I let her guide me back out to the road.

I dream of a battered flysheet, torn loose by the wind, winding up and up into the sky. So far up, I am afraid to turn back and look down. This time I do not resist the dream. I do not wake myself in protest. I just go up and up, following the sheet, until we are both no more than tiny specks against the clouds.

When the dream is over, I go on yielding. Now to sleep's stochastic release. I'm in the sitting room that shares a wall with my mother's bedroom in the flat on Eighty-First Street. The torn olive settee smells of feet. Then I'm in a college dorm reeking of formaldehyde and wondering what happened to the doughy girl who dropped out after we slept together. Then home. The wide bed. Clarissa's morning hair, fizzy gold against the cotton sheets. I lean in quick to touch her before she is gone. Only the bed, huge and cold around me. Then a lumpy single bed, the one I fell into last night. No map that puts all these places together except the girl. The one who was not Olivia.

Water roars and a kettle bleats like a harmonica.

I open my eyes to see Alexandra stooped over the stove in a green silk robe, pouring water into a French press.

"How'd you get my number?"

"You awake?" she asks.

"I never give out my cell. How'd you find it?"

"On the back of your business card, hand-written. Could barely read it so I guessed it was yours. Doctor's scrawl."

"What time is it?"

"Almost noon. I called your office, told them you were sick."

I leap up, keeping the blanket wrapped around me. I'm in an old T-shirt. Hers. It smells faintly muggy. I feel strangely small inside of it.

"Rest. They'll live. You look exhausted."

It was an experiment, coming here, borrowing her shirt, not taking off to places I know will cater to me. "I've got to be back by two. Surgery."

"You'll never make it. They can have lipo another day."

I don't have time to argue. I get up and head to the bathroom. The fan and light are burnt out. A tiny window sheds dim light. My clothes hang neatly behind the door. I throw them on. I'll shower at the clinic.

Alexandra knocks, then opens the door just enough to push a cup through. "Slow down. They'll live one day without you." She makes it sound so easy, like my clients haven't arranged their entire lives around today's schedule.

The cup is warm in my hand. The coffee smells rich and spicy. I take a sip.

"You called the office and talked to Sandy?" I come back into the kitchen.

"She was dubious. She asked what appointments you wanted to cancel. I had to tell her the day's lineup before she believed me."

"You searched my bag?"

She shrugs, "Your calendar was on the counter, you emptied stuff out last night."

I see my bag sitting wide open beside her. She's right, I was looking for my phone before bed. I think about calling Sandy and how to explain. She'll have the day cleared by now. Everything rescheduled. Doesn't matter how fast I move, I'll arrive at an empty office.

Alexandra sits on the edge of the bed. It's not really a bed but a foam pad that folds up into a chair. Her place is spare. The kitchen is a small galley that looks out to the living room with its shabby couch and thinning carpet. Cookbooks are stacked on the breakfast bar and lush green plants drape down from a shelf above a glass patio door where the last of the morning breeze blows through.

"You can't just reorganize my life," I tell her.

"What if you were sick? You'd cancel."

"I don't get sick." I sit next to her, take another sip. She's impossible. Still, it's done. Useless getting riled.

Alexandra drains her cup, swallows hard, "I was up half the night."

I nod. I slept straight through but it doesn't feel like it.

"Do you think she was afraid?" she looks at me. Her eyes are watery.

"All those drugs in her? She can't have been feeling much at all." Some girl overdosed at a party. Her friends, if they could be called that, panicked and dumped her body out by the lake. I stand and move to a stool by the kitchen bar.

Alexandra follows me, refills our cups from the white plastic drip on the counter.

"But she must have known she was dying. We do, when it's time."

"I don't like to think about it."

She searches my face for a moment then says, "Occupational hazard?" I shrug, not understanding. She lets me flounder, then offers a wry smile, "You're a cosmetic surgeon. You cheat age, death's wake up call."

I don't know whether she is mocking or teasing me. She keeps on watching to see what I will say. One minute she is dreamy and the next she is sly. I can't quite make her out. An odd mix.

"Not really. You can't cheat death. If you insist on looking at it that way, I simply help turn a blind eye."

She laughs, "True," then turns to stare out to the patio. Her thigh peeks out from the robe's satin edge, muscular and sinuous above a rough-hewn knee. She reaches down and smoothes the robe back.

It's only noon and the day's already suffocating. I can smell yesterday's sweat in my clothes.

"Do you mind if I shower? It was a long drive, a long day." She dips her head in a nod.

The showerhead spews a dismal, tepid stream. I should just go into town and check into a hotel. Something about Alexandra keeps catching me off guard. I'm doing things I'd never do. The water smells of sulfur and chlorine. How can she stand this place? A waste out here where there's nothing going on. She seems smart, intuitive, competent.

When I'm done, water keeps dribbling out of the tub spout and down a worn patch in the enamel. I pull the water on again and shut it off. It was dry when I got in, but no matter what I do, the tepid stream won't stop. I yank the faucet, then ram with force.

The enclosure shudders. The tap, still gripped by my fist, disappears inside the wall. Water spews everywhere. I call out, but Alexandra is already there. She throws me a towel, pulls me from the room, and leaves while I dry off.

She must have found the water main because I hear everything stop. When I look in, water drips down the walls, the floor is flooded, my clothes drenched. I throw some extra towels down, start to mop up.

The towel around my waist is soaked but I pull it up, wrap myself in it when I hear Alexandra's step. My hair clings to my face in damp clumps.

I try to apologize, but she shirks it off, "Look at the rot." She points to the hole. "It was bound to happen eventually." She takes me in from head to foot. "What a mess," she laughs and nods toward her bedroom. "Go see what I have that fits you."

Wrapped in the towel, I sneak out to my car and dig workout clothes from my gym bag. It's late, even for lunch, but I make a fresh pot of coffee, scramble us some eggs, and make toast.

The plumber is an old codger. Shorn speckled hair pokes out from his grubby cap. His belly stretches against faded, blotchy overalls. He takes a good long time pulling up linoleum, tapping at the walls. He pulls out a cigarette, doesn't look at us, and says it'll be at least a week before he can start. That there'll be more to do. The wall joists are pretty bad. The floor beneath could be a problem. Could be weeks to get everything lined up and back in working order.

He ties off the shower head and faucet so that the water can be turned back on. His bill is two hundred dollars. After some fuss on my part, Alexandra lets me pay.

I'm guessing the cost will be in the thousands, maybe more by the look of that rot, but I'm not sure she knows that yet.

It is impulsive of me, we hardly know each other. "Please," I say, "come stay at my place."

"It's not your fault."

"I have plenty of room. The house is too big for one. Please, just pack some things and come."

She meets my gaze dead on, face frozen, eyes glassy, then hands the plumber a key and goes into the bedroom. I hear her opening and shutting drawers.

I give him my address, "You can send the bills here. Do you know anyone who can help with the rest?"

"I might. Most guys I know are pretty busy though."

"Tell them there's a bonus in it for anyone who can start within a week. Another for all of you if it's done before the month's out. Three weeks. Can we can get this sorted out by then?"

Two cancellations in a row this morning. I pour myself a cup of tea. Always with no-shows it's tea, not coffee, which emphasizes the waiting, and reading the journals I can never keep up with.

Morning haze from the ocean wraps the windows in muslin. A soothing treat to mark the approach of fall. The tick of the clock measures this moment and then another. Each beat now, over and over again. Rain on mosaic tiles. I kick off my shoes and tuck my legs up beside me on the couch. The words knot on the page. I trace the lines of desk from the floor to its glossy surface with light pooled on top.

Perhaps it is time to open the room up. A pair of soft rose colored chairs, a small table between, an offering of tea, coffee, or glass of something cool. Nothing structural. Just a little redecorating to make clients feel more at home.

I think about the no-shows, try to remember their faces. Do they regret not coming? Where are they now? Are they thinking that they should be here? That it's something they've always wanted but can't have?

The haze has turned to mist. The light is held inside and noise of the traffic is muffled. I see myself reflected in the window. The woman in the glass looks peaceful. She gazes out at me and I feel the warmth of waiting, like bathwater filling in around me. Only the torpid sound of the ticking clock. The woman remains in the glass, moving neither into nor out of the room, watching, always watching from the place that exists only here, in this room when the light shines just like it is right now. The sound of the clock gets louder and further away and the succession of seconds grows slick, slipping out from beneath me.

I close my eyes, let myself ease down, bring the woman in the window with me to the dream. The woman smiles like she knows a thing that has already happened, a long time back, the thing for which we are waiting. I move to the glass and put my hand against it. Cool from the mist.

Then I am outside in the feathery drizzle. The city roads jut away in jagged lines, between clustered shops, a newsstand, a small, steepled church, a bus stop. All of them empty and closed. The air smells dark, but it is day. I wander from the square. At each bend in the road, the pattern of the city repeats itself—the bus stop, a small steepled church, closed clusters of shops. It is not comforting. I keep walking down one path to another and another.

Then I get there. The small shop with its hanging wooden sign and red door locked up tight. No light in the storefront. I think this is where the woman lived, or lived when the thing happened that we are waiting for. The shop looks smaller than I thought it would. Old and less romantic than I remembered, with the smell of damp in the wood. The key is in my pocket, and I go in.

An unmade bed in the corner with white sheets and thick comforter bunched up in folds of silk and merlot velvet. An impression of where one head lay in a soft pillow and the hint of another. Cold ash in the fireplace. I undress. My skin puckers with cold. The sound of the sea. I am near the edge of the town, out by the water where the pattern that goes on and on ends.

I sit on the edge of the bed, tuck my hands beneath my bare thighs, and wait. The sea is loud.

When the man comes, she comes in through the door and lies down beneath a single layer of sheet on the bed. The warmth of her curving body muffles the cold. I could turn and lay her body on top, take him inside, turn her inside out, the way I have a thousand times, so that our bodies fall together, inward to the smallest point. But there is the sound of the sea and the smell of musk and the room is cold, as if it is something that has happened long ago.

Even when the roof opens and the sky gives way, there is the long wash upward to the room with the clock ticking and the haze breaking. I cannot release the heat of her. The moment is detached, and I am held inside of it, like the woman in the pane of glass.

Someone taps on the door.

"Eleanor?" Alexandra opens it and peeks in "Sandy said you were alone and I could come on back. You okay? I thought we could go for lunch."

She looks magnificent. Draped in a simple, undyed linen shift that elegantly accentuates her height, angular shoulders, and narrow hips, her face pink and glowing above a saffron and carmine silk scarf. Her hair is combed back and tied like a halo around her face. So different from people I usually see here. Vibrant, outlined discretely in some way I can't quite put my finger on. I blink and look away.

"How did you get here?"

"I caught a ride into town."

"I need a moment—"

"Were you sleeping? Are you okay?"

"I'll be with you in a minute."

Alexandra closes the door without a sound. Her footsteps retreat. The day is growing brighter. The room reorders itself into the place that it was before. Everything as it should be. The sound of the clock disappears into the whoosh of passing traffic. A horn bleats, a truck rattles, a seagull cries.

The next morning, Sandy hands me the air conditioning maintenance bill, "They went a bit over."

"How much?"

"Just a little more than their contract."

"Well, at least it's done." The clinic is the perfect temperature again. The air feels clean and cool.

"There's a client here already. No appointment. Shall I send her back when she comes out?" I nod. "She's in the bathroom." Sandy gazes at me with meaning. "It's Asa, the one with the eyelid? Says she just wants a few minutes."

"She's back? We fixed it. No charge, right? What does she want?"

"Looks like she's been through the wringer. Her face is scratched up and she seems pretty fragile. Said it was some kind of accident, but see for yourself. I didn't press."

I go back to my office and wait. Asa comes in and huddles up tight in the loveseat. I move toward her slowly, ask if I may examine her cuts. Handmade by the look of them. They run down her face from beneath her eyes to the base of her jaw. Like someone went at her in a frenzy. A terrified child? Horrible to imagine. She won't tell me what happened when I ask. I hesitate to put my hands to her face. Suddenly afraid my touch, my manner, will not be right for such a delicate situation. Then I think, if it's strength and confidence she needs, too much hesitation will sour everything. When I touch her brow, she straightens up, and looks me in the eye. Her face flushes with warmth. I smile gently and tell her the wounds are healing just fine.

She asks if she can come back for more consultation once she heals. Again, I hesitate. It may be more than she can handle, but in the end I say okay.

The next time I see Asa, she is animated. Stepping brightly into the room, she sits forward on the loveseat. She wears a bright pink-orange blazer. Her eyes flash feverishly. Her fingers fly up to her face and flutter against her cheeks. "You see here, where they are so flat? I want something more pronounced."

I lean back in my chair, fold my fingers into a steeple. She is a different woman since I saw her last. The scratch marks are almost gone. She's so animated and alive. The new, pink skin nearly blends with her natural flush. I'm delighted by the change. Did she come back because she wanted me to see? Because I was part of it? Odd, though, that she's here. She's nearly healed physically, but emotionally she must still be working things through.

"Why?" I ask. "What is it you hope to achieve?"

I never ask my clients why. They expect me to know, to understand when maybe no one else does.

She looks at me for the longest time, hands clasped tight over her knees, face still and earnest.

"I feel like I've never been loved."

I am silent for a moment. It is not what I expected. Clients give hundreds of reasons, but this one is the root of so many. I have thought this for a long time, but never said so. That Asa does, surprises me.

"You've been through a lot. Have you talked things out with someone close, a friend, perhaps a counselor?" My suggestions seem pathetic. Once the maw of loneliness is owned, which of these gives any real solace?

Asa's demeanor remains expectant. She speaks slowly and carefully, as if explaining to a child. "I've done a lot of thinking. Years and years of it."

"I'm not sure surgery is the way forward," I say.

"It's like I'm a run-down motel room." She talks faster now, "You know what I mean? You must. You must see this all the time. At best, people come and have a look. Then they go find somewhere better."

We watch each other for a few moments. What can I say? That I know? Or is it more professional to lie and pretend I don't? When I say nothing she goes on.

"Let me just tell you what I am thinking of. I can see it in my mind like it's real." She massages her cheeks, "High and round with a good hollow space beneath so that my eyes do not look so beady. And my brow is too flat. Do you see?"

Of course I see. I nod, suddenly curious. How does she know this would go with the cheeks? How has she envisioned something so complete? Asa is different in a way that wakes me up.

"Can you show me? It is easier to see examples." I hand her a book of models and photos of famous people. I want to know if there is someone she is basing this on. Some star in the limelight or one of the new trends. She takes it, and then she eyes the coffee table and pulls off my portfolio. The book is heavy, full of years of work. The section on cheeks itself is three inches thick.

"See the way this one sits high?" She points to a woman who looks nothing like her. "See the hollow there?"

She goes on for quite a while, through each section: eyes, ears, noses, lips, brows, cheeks. When she finds something that seems right, she slips in a little piece of green paper torn from something crumpled in her purse.

"Can you tell me why you want so much change, all at once?" Most clients create big changes little by little, one step at a time.

"Do you ever feel like something's way off, and no matter what you do, you can't make it right? I mean what you see, something is just not the way you see it in your head?"

Nodding, I almost answer. I nearly laugh then catch myself. She's avoiding the question. "But so much change," I press.

"Yes! Change. That's it. So hopeful, don't you think?"

"How do you mean?" I ask. She gets that vague little smile like the first time she was here.

"I mean so much can happen, things you have no control over. But this is different. This has purpose, takes careful planning, the both of us figuring it out together. That's hopeful, don't you think?"

We don't set up surgery. I tell her I want to go over what we've discussed, analyze what might be possible, and that I will get back to her with recommendations. She seems pleased with my answer, so I let it go at that.

When she leaves, I am still curious. That evening, after surgery, I go back through the book she's marked. All past clients. I have their images and Asa's stored electronically. I load them in the software and start to cut and paste.

When it is all there, I tweak the topography of the grid. Shrinking the scale here, enlarging it there, incrementally shifting the virtual undulations of the face. With each minute change, I toggle to the image. Little by little, cheeks lift. Faint, shadowy hollows appear beneath, accentuating the eyes exquisitely.

It would be a big project, a challenge. I'm glad I have photos from the beginning. *Cosmetics Quarterly* might even be interested in doing an article. But there would be so little left of Asa. Is she ready for so much change? Can she handle it?

I stop. Look closely at the screen, and something begins to surface. I tweak the contour more gradually now, watching the image as it comes into focus. Until it is her. The girl. Olivia.

Aged by twenty years.

The house is lit when I arrive. I stand for a moment in the tiled entry, listening for Alexandra. She's been holing up here nearly six weeks. Except for the lights, she never leaves signs of life. She does not set her books out on the coffee table. No dirty cups on the kitchen sink. No hair collecting on the floor of the guest bathroom. The bed in the spare room remade each day. If anything, the house is more spotless than when I leave in the morning.

No one in the kitchen. A wineglass and a clean plate are set out with a pink sticky note that says "Dinner in the fridge!" A stack of three, square Tupperware containers sits on the lowest shelf. I fill the glass and stand at the counter, running my fingers up and down the cold stone.

"That you?" Her voice drifts in from the patio. "Back here."

I don't want to go. My face must look as leaden as it feels. I just need a drink and a quiet, dark room with nothing in it. I fix two gins, knock one back, and pour another.

I do not look at her, just hand her a glass, fall into the chaise, and stare up into the cool October sky. The stars are coming out.

"Long day?"

"Mmmm, wanted to catch up. Sorry, I should have called."

"That would have been nice. You said you'd be home tonight, so I made dinner."

"I'm sorry. I completely forgot."

She sighs.

"What?"

"Its just . . . Can I ask? Did you do this kind of thing with Clarissa?"

"What kind of thing?"

"You keep talking about how neurotic she was about keeping appointments and being late. But you kind of act like yours is the only time that matters. I'm just a houseguest, and it doesn't feel good."

"I didn't think being at home tonight was important."

"Ah," she says, her face turned up to the sky.

I don't answer. "How's the construction going?"

Her eyes light. "The room looks great. You should go see."

"I meant at your place."

"I couldn't get hold of anyone today. Must be on another job." She waves her hand through the air, brushing the thought away.

"You can't let them get away with that. You need to stay on them or it will never be done."

"I will. I'll call tomorrow."

"You have to keep pushing. If you don't, they'll jerk you around."

"What's got you riled? Clarissa? I shouldn't have brought her up."

"I try not to think about it. She's decided to go for broke. Take me to court and see if she can get half of everything."

I want to tell her the rest. How I created Olivia's face from bits and pieces of others, like a monster, a beautiful cyborg living in my head. I keep seeing her, now I'm making her from scratch. Crazy. Like if I could bring her back, start it over, set that one day right. Then maybe everything that came after would be different.

"She'll never make it stick."

"You'd be surprised." I should let it spill, tell her everything that's really going on, all about Asa and Olivia and how things that should be separate keep leaking into each other. But I don't. I tell myself it's because I don't talk about clients. I make it my business to keep everything strictly confidential. In truth, though, I've broken that rule a lot. I force myself to think about Clarissa. I don't like it, but it's something I can grab hold of. "Precedents are being set. I think she likes the idea of being part of that."

"What grounds does she have?!"

I tell her about how things are changing. One judge might give Clarissa nothing and another could give her half. The crapshoot of progress. But, as I talk, all the while I'm thinking of the office, how I'm glad the image of Olivia is there, saved so I can come back to it later.

She listens to all of it and when I run out of things to say, she stands, shakes her head as if at nonsense—the world's, not mine—and goes inside to open a bottle of wine. When I'm alone, I want her to come back, to lean up against her like that night out at the lake, and let exhaustion take me over. She knows the perfect time to leave the room, to let me sit and think before I say something I'll regret. Because of her discretion, I want to tell her more, about work and the girl, but it's more than I know how to begin.

When she returns, she reaches for my hand.

"Come. See the room."

I follow her through the house. It feels like that dream where I walk down a road that repeats itself over and over and I never go out to the edge to see where it stops, where things might be different. When we get there, she reaches for the door and then throws it wide.

"Magnificent!"

"What did they do?" I really can't tell the difference from when I stuck my head in a while back. Although somehow it does look neater and more finished.

"The trim. Jesus, El. They sweated over the miter for days. Look at these joins!" She runs her finger over a corner where the baseboards meet. "Spot on, everywhere. It's gorgeous!"

Well, of course they'd join, I want to say. I'm paying enough.

"It will look better once you get stuff in. You could do it more modern than the rest. All those great, sleek lines in the windows."

"I think I should tear it out."

"Start over?!"

"No. Just rip it down."

"Don't touch it. Don't make them take one more thing apart! It's perfect as it is. Plus, if you touch it, you'll have a revolt on your hands. You should hear what they say when you're not around."

"Like?"

"It's hard to take your own work apart. They're demoralized."

I think of them, sweaty and grumpy with foul names for me on their lips. Even the small one. Especially her. It was not meant to be this way. Just something to do. Something to watch take shape.

But I can't undo it. I can't go back. I have to keep moving forward. Make the best out of it I can. Alexandra is walking around the room, entranced with details I can't even see. She blooms here, like I knew she would. But it doesn't give me pleasure to see I was right.

"If you can see how to make it work, knock yourself out." I turn from the room.

"Really?"

"You decorate it, I'll pay your construction bills." It's not like I can afford to add her bills to mine. But she can't afford them either, and all I know is I don't want her to go. I can't stand to be alone even if I go on shutting her out.

"God! I'd love . . . You wouldn't have to pay me."

"Just make it right, okay? Just fix the damn thing."

The next day, I go in early to look at the images again. I want to start over with the parts and make them come out different. The girl does not belong in all this, that much is obvious. I will not go on being haunted by her. I will move on, let her go. This project is just one more way to face things head on, get back to the present.

Before my first client arrives, Sandy buzzes to say Eugenie Taylor's in. Her surgery is scheduled for the afternoon.

I close down the software and save my progress. It's promising, in a way. I think I can make a different look for Asa. And disturbing. It really was just my own imagination that made the girl appear. I have to pull myself together, straighten myself out, get back to the no-nonsense Eleanor clients expect.

Eugenie's been with me for years. If anything can set me back on course, it's the habitual calming of her preoperative dramas. She bursts in and splays three photos of noses in front of me.

"How about these?" finger jabbing at the photos, her bulk swaying over me.

Each nose has been carefully clipped away from the rest of the photo. The blobs swim across the desk as if searching for the rest of their faces. But I still recognize them. One belongs to that straw-blonde actress recently skyrocketing to fame, another to the governor's wife, the last could belong to just about anyone who's had her nose done in the last six months.

"Look, we've been over this." My voice is sharp. I take a breath and start again as if I'm calm, "We decided the course of action weeks ago. If you want to change plans, I'm not doing it day of surgery. We need time to think it through."

Eugenie's eyes narrow and her mouth twists into a puffy rosette. She won't want to put off the operation. Not when it's so close. In her mind, transformation has already begun. To delay will choke the dream and perhaps throw a delicately balanced social calendar in havoc.

"Are you sure I don't need something more pert and youthful?"

"Trust me." I stare her down until she looks at the photos wistfully, releasing the noses and the dazzling faces that remained attached no matter how scrupulously she clipped. She will praise me, as she always does after these fits of doubt, and tell her friends that my skill is well worth the cost. She admires the price tag as much as the work, although I've begun to suspect it is well beyond her means. Sandy mentioned something about payments past due.

She gathers the pictures up in her hand and crumples them. "Well, I guess you know what you're doing. I mean that's what I pay you for, right?"

I nod. Eugenie already has the perfect Aegean nose to balance her olive-shaped eyes and firm, unyielding lips. It is simply set a little too far forward. Besides this one last task, the beauty I have excavated from her face is classic, eternal. The noses she brought in are modern and common. I am disappointed, after all this time working together, that she doesn't get it.

I can't help but think again of Asa, how she has an eye for what works together. Not many clients could pick out pieces to make a coherent face. So much more invigorating than working with clients like Eugenie. If I can keep steering away from my own regrets, I can see the promise of it. Asa would have a new face, a stunning new beginning. Seems like she deserves that. We all do sometimes, need a new start.

If I can just get Olivia out of my head, what Asa has in mind could work.

When I see Eugenie again, she is already out. I had the anesthesiologist take care of that. No arguments on the table. The knife slides up the right nostril and, with the slightest pressure, slips the skin apart. Thank god she came to me from the start. Errors on the nose can be particularly difficult to fix. The scissors can catch and tear the skin. Gently, I open a medial marginal incision of the columella, releasing the skin from cartilage.

One twitch could mar the lower lateral cartilages. Nasal lobes can fuse with scarring. I have corrected enough of my colleagues' errors to know the dangers. Skill requires vigilance. The line between success and failure is finer than most like to admit.

I cut across the base of the columella, that proud column of flesh that separates the nostrils, and ease the skin back from the nose. Naked, white mounds of cartilage come into full view. Eugenie's are something to behold. Pronounced, perfectly symmetrical, thrusting gracefully from the opening, they are not her problem.

It is the projection of the anterior nasal spine that causes the nose to sit too far forward. Other surgeons would have missed this and savagely hacked away at the faultless domes of cartilage. The bone protrudes where the base of the nose meets the top of the upper lip, extending the length of the nose and pushing it too far from the surface of the face. The projection must be chiseled from the skull.

I explained to Eugenie that the procedure is irreversible. With bone, I am careful to emphasize this. The original shape may be reengineered, but that is simply another alteration that may or may not succeed.

I set the chisel to the tip of the nasal spine, measuring off three-eighths of an inch on the offending protrusion. This extra bone that pushes the nose from the surface of the face is a genetic trait. A tiny triangle, handed down through generations from the genetic mix of ancestors long dead. A family insignia. As specific as a coat of arms.

I draw the chisel across, etch a line and then tap. The scrap falls free.

My hand hovers. The cartilage mottles pink. I examine the ragged white fleck at the scalpel's tip. Where it was attached, the cut is smooth and flat. The remaining bone is sculpted exactly as planned. The adjustment will be a success. But the edge of bone on the blade, the one that once pushed against the septum's posterior cartilage, is irregular, lopsided. I keep looking at it. So jagged and imperfect.

Strange.

I have the urge to slip it into my scrubs pocket. Like finding a shark's tooth on the beach.

I stay late again. Finishing Asa's new images engrosses me. I am finding my way out of something I couldn't before. With each adjustment, I stop and consider the surgical techniques that would make it possible. It is well past midnight when I finally decide to shut down. I will come up with a plan, a timeline, an estimated cost. Then I'll sit on this a while. I want to consider the client carefully. Is she ready? Can she bare the strain? Am I the right one to make that call? I'm still not sure what I should do, but I save it all in a new file under Asa's name.

Alexandra

Last November, Olivia shows up out of nowhere. She sets up in the lake dunes, out by old shacks half-submerged and falling down. We all leave her alone. Some college kid getting her head together. She'll be gone by Monday. Debris spills from the city to the bright desert winter all the time.

On Monday afternoon, it rains. Slim winter light shimmies in between sky and lake. Everything smells of quickened soil. Her floppy little tent is still pitched against the sand as the night turns cold.

Before bed, I wrap up in a wool shawl, a long skirt and warm leggings, and take a flask of tea and leftovers. I go the long route from my place out along the shore. She's made a dismal little campfire from trash and pieces of rotted shack. Her hair is lank and her face grubby. I sit and she starts talking, tense and sarcastic, like she was tired of waiting for someone to come.

She offers me a smoke. Mostly she talks about the city. She talks all in past tense. Her knee jiggles up and down.

"I mean, it was fucking all about looking good and acting like life was great, one stinking day after another. I fucking had to get out." Her sentences end with periods, but nothing she says sounds certain.

She's going to think I'm an old fart, but so what?—I say: "You seem like a good kid." She does. "You're smart, good-looking. And I think you know it, too."

"Good kid is different from good-looking." Her glare is fragile. She's hasn't been on her own for long. "How I look has nothing to do with me."

By the light of stars, a close circle of fireweed and clumps of new grasses wave in a steady breeze. Beyond them is the bare glow of the lake.

"No one gets that," she says. "Most of all my mother." She fiddles with the sleeve of her sweatshirt. She is tall and slender. The shirt is baggy and loose.

I know we're on safer ground, now. Someone at home, waiting.

I ask her, but all she'll tell me is that her mother is broken up inside, and she's only made it worse. There was no other way, she says, and she asks me why that is.

"I don't know."

I come back the next night, and she is quiet. Asks me to tell her a story from when I was little.

So I tell her how I used to imagine I was flying from one land to another across a bright blue sea. She listens, in that same intent way she speaks. I tell her that I flew and flew until I was sure I'd never make it back, but still couldn't see land in front. The more I talk, the more I remember how it was to not have words for things that I knew.

I tell her that I had wings tattooed on my back when I turned twenty-one. She wants to see them. I say no, it was a long time ago. I say they are not as beautiful as they had been on my young, firm skin. She asks me to describe them and, as I do, she crawls into her tent and falls asleep to the sound of my voice.

Later on, she comes by the house and asks again, could she please see the wings.

It's raining hard. The water runs down her legs and into her canvas shoes. She hugs herself, shivering. I tell her no, but I let her in.

I put the kettle on, give her a robe to change into, and ask her if it's okay if I pop her jeans and sweatshirt in the wash. They're caked with grime and mud. She nods. I love rain at the lake. In the winter, the skies open. Pocked dirt and muddy rivulets flashing through old gullies. The lake's surface boils. Angles blur and the light draws in close. She looks like a child in my robe. Maybe nine or ten, trapped in a body growing up.

I watch her curl up tight on the couch. Cheeks flushed, face expectant.

What is she doing out here on her own?

"You're not going to see what you think."

She looks down at her bare feet and then tucks them beneath the robe. Her mouth pushes together in a pout. Then she looks at me straight on, her eyes grey in the muted light, her face older, sorrowful. "I get it. You're in the wrong body. Me too."

I sit and think for a moment, because it seems important that I answer right. Then I say, "No. It's all mine. It's never been any other way for me."

I want to ask her more about what she meant, but she frowns and scoots away as if I have rebuffed her. So I tell her. "I'm still male, in the way most people know men as male. I never wanted that to change. But I'm entirely female, the way I know female. Hormones help. Other than that, my body's the way it's always been, the way I was born. It seems odd, I know. But I'm not trapped in the wrong body. What I have is completely natural to me, it's my own, my own female body."

She nods and looks at me in that mute, paralyzed way people do when they want to say something, but they can only think of things they're scared will come out wrong. She wraps her arms around her chest then rolls her eyes. "So are you going to let me see the tattoo or what?" a half smirk. She's used to getting her way.

I go into my bedroom and sit at the edge of my bed. She seems to need something, but I don't think it's this. I don't think I'm who, or what, she's looking for.

I watch my reflection in the mirror as I undress then pull a long cotton wrap around my shoulders, draping it over my back and covering my chest. I go out to the living room, sit on the couch, and she pops up from the floor to join me. I turn away from her.

She scoots close, and I feel her warmth behind me. I lift the wrap from my back.

She puts her finger on my spine. Her touch moves up my back and then out across each shoulder blade, tracing the outlines of imaginary feathers. The tattoo was just an idea, one I played with for years, then let fade. Rain runs down the windows, muffling noise. Everything inside sounds nearer: the tick of the clock, the radiator clicking, the hum of the refrigerator. She moves her palms, as if combing quills into place. Her hands are small and nimble. An unfamiliar heat rises in my skin, blood rushing along the path of her touch.

When Olivia leaves town, she doesn't say goodbye. I go out one morning, and the tent is gone. I ask around, but no one knows where she went or when.

A couple weeks later, flyers go up about a runaway at Millie's corner store and on the board at the Salty Dog. The police don't come out. They have my name, but other things come up.

Four-year-old twins missing in Cochilla, a rash of teenage thieving in Borrego Springs. High drama for out here in the desert.

I think about her months later, when I am getting ready to go to the city with Eleanor. It's harder to go than I thought.

I don't want to. But things happen and sometimes you have to just follow them out to see where they end up.

I stop to see Mary on my way out of town.

"L.A.? You're going to the city?" She's at the register. Her short, plump body is tucked neatly into jeans and a flannel shirt.

"I can't help it, poppet. Don't be mad."

"I'm not mad, I just think the city's crazy. It'll eat you up. Like those big machines in the shows kids watch. Made up of a million pieces that come apart and go back together different." She tugs on a wayward strand of her tight, black curls. "Too much to keep track of."

"It's not the city. It's something else," I nod toward Eleanor's slick, black car. Mary looks, but we can't see inside the dark windows. "Think of me as a scientist. I want to know her habitat."

"Science? It's the open door you love. Through the wardrobe. That kind of thing."

"Maybe, but it beats being impaled by summer heat while I watch construction workers trash my place."

"Well, go then. Send me a postcard from Venice Beach or something. But don't be a stranger."

We laugh instead of saying goodbye.

I feel a little sad leaving her behind. Sometimes the only way to know how attached you are is to lift up and go.

On the drive, I watch the way the desert looses its grip. Small blooms of box houses, gas stations, and fast food places take hold. Eventually, nothing much but cement. A few brown lawns and scraggly trees are all that hint at the idea of soil. So many angles, surfaces, letter fonts, street widths. The details pile up. Too many to take in. Too distinct to blur. It's overwhelming. I wonder if I've done the right thing. Here I am in the car with someone who's almost a stranger, headed back to a city full of strangers. Makes me wonder if I know myself.

Eleanor sits up tall and talks almost the whole way, her hands animated. They move on and off the wheel. I settle back and watch her. I like the way she moves—graceful and precise—even when she's rambling. Something about watching her makes me think everything will be okay, that I am taking this trip for a reason—I just don't know what it is yet. She's still talking and I hear parts, but not all, of what she says:

"Clinic on Santa Monica Boulevard."

"Maybe *Vanity Fair* next year."

"The remodel's close to done."

"Clarissa." Then a little silence before she moves on to something else.

Her words drift around me. So much city flashing by, it's hard to focus. When we hit the coast, Eleanor slows down, eases back in her seat, looks out at the ocean, and stops talking. We turn onto the long winding road that climbs up between rock and oak and fences with horses grazing behind. We arrive just before dark.

Everything here is immaculate, like its owner. No stains on the white wool Berber. When Eleanor throws open the windows and doors to a light breeze, no dust bunnies tumble out from the graceful lines of the French country antiques. A place of perfect calm. Especially the new addition. She explains disdainfully, running her hands over her narrow waist, "It's my cross to bear, I guess."

The room's a triangle that slopes up and out toward the sky. The walls and windows are framed, but there is no drywall or doors. The hills outside look like Italy, brown and green, rolling and dotted with cypress, the blue sea at their feet.

She has changed into fresh clothes. Slim black jeans and a white polo shirt. She stands just inside the door and leans back, arms folded, against the wall.

"It's gorgeous. Here, and the rest of the house," I say.

"You get used to it. After a while, all you see is what doesn't quite work."

"Well, it's not done yet."

"I can tell already." With one step, she moves from the room, and I follow.

"If you've decided already you won't like it, then you're not really giving it a chance."

"It's called foresight."

Most mornings Eleanor flies out of her bedroom, grabs a quick breakfast or nothing at all, and goes off to work. Sometimes I sleep in. The guest room is set back, away from the main part of the house. I don't even hear her go. I have the place to myself mostly. During the day, I sit by the pool, go through her closets, browse her art books. I thought I'd want to go downtown, to the Fairfax District to see if anyone I knew was still around. I went through the phonebook, but it's hard to tell. People move. Names change. Canter's is still there. I could go in for a bite and ask around. But I don't.

I go to the beach, Santa Monica, the old Getty. I send Mary some stuff on Pompeii and archeology for kids. Mostly though, I just want to be at the house where it's quiet, and I can look out at the hills.

The city makes me anxious. It's a shock to find it all still here, going on without me. In the afternoons, I make dinner and set the table. Just a little something to make us both feel more at home. The weeks start slipping by. Before I know it, I've been here almost a month.

One morning the doorbell rings. A drab, little woman stands in the bright sun. Her hair is tied back tightly in glinting silver butterfly clips. Her face painted in strained pinks. She wears a coral blazer that is a size too large. But what seems most out of place is the wide, toothy smile that cracks her face in two.

"I'm in the neighborhood today representing Oh-Cosmetics. Completely allergy free, not tested on animals, made to protect and pamper your skin." She pats her shiny metal box case. "I was wondering if I could introduce you to our products."

"No." I look past her down the driveway. It's maybe a quarter mile between houses out here. Is she walking? I don't see a car. She's wearing heels. Her feet bulge from the black leather straps. Must be parked just down past the bend.

"It's free of cost or obligation."

I step back and put my hand on the door. It is enormous, solid in my hand, heavy on its hinges. I start to pull it closed, but she goes on as if she hasn't noticed. "I have a number of free samples you might like."

She stands unmoving in the arched entryway. I like the way she looks at me, as if I'm the obstacle she has to overcome to make a sale. Another rich, lazy woman, holding the purse strings. She just has to find the right way to get a piece for herself. I like being the one standing in her way.

"You can come in. Just for a few minutes. I'm very busy."

She moves quickly now, her legs jerking into motion as she teeters on her heels. She pauses at the threshold of the living room, taking it in. It really is spectacular—tall white bookcases filled with a tasteful display of literature, art books, and a collection of small bronzes. There's a wide, muslin-colored sofa and matching chairs around a glass table and pale pink oriental rug. Nothing is ostentatious. No silk curtains with flouncy valances or veiny marble surfaces. Just classic, high-quality stuff put together with an eye for shape and shadow.

The woman stops, sighs, and turns back to me, "My name's Bunny." She extends a plucky arm.

"Alexandra."

"It's a beautiful home. You must love being here all day." She drops my hand after the briefest touch.

She is strange and edgy. I wish I hadn't invited her in. Still, the idea that I live here, on my own terms. . . . I've always been happy with what I have. Or, at least I've been good at making due. Grateful for the little nest egg my uncle left me when he died. But Eleanor has an eye for things. The kind of things folks like to see looking back at them. That's why she does well in her line of work.

Bunny can't stop taking it in. She goes to the bookcases and looks over the titles, then to the bronzes, then over to the windows and gazes out at the pool. She does this all quickly, eagerly. Then she comes and sits stiffly on the couch, kitty-corner from me. She opens her case on the table and stares into my face with a hard little smile on her lips.

"Can I get you coffee?" My cup is still in my hand; the coffee is cold.

"I try to avoid it. Bad for the skin. I could use water, though."

When I come back, she is up again, examining the botanical prints on the far wall. Her shoulders square as she hears my footstep on the stair, a little block of coral pink floating against the white walls.

When she sits this time, she places herself across from me on the other side of the glass table. She rests her hand on the case and peers at me intently, "Autumn, right?" I nod.

Amazing how when someone thinks you have money they give you things for free. Despite her stiff demeanor, she leaves the good stuff, not just sample-sized. Sun block foundation from France, thick, dark liner, a robust blush. The last is a little more orange than I'd choose, but I don't complain.

"I don't usually give this out," she says about the foundation. "Use it for a week, and you'll see improvement in the skin. I do. Covers every flaw. It's made with MMP Inhibitors, Hyperdermal Destressors." She squints at the label. "All the latest technology. It's new on the market. I think you'll like it." She drops the tube in my open hand, stands, smiles primly, and runs her ruddy hands once down the front of her jacket.

"Sure is a nice place you've got. Bet you know folks who'd just move right in if they could."

I shake my head.

She smiles broadly and points a blunt finger at me laughing but not friendly, "Gotta watch out for those kind of friends, huh?"

Neither of us smile at the joke. What's she playing at? I don't like her much. I watch from the door as she walks down the drive. I hear the sound of a car starting up and driving off down the hill. Must have started at the top. Working her way down. A schlep of a job. No wonder she's got an edge. I head on into the guest bathroom to try the stuff out.

In the mirror, I am surprised to see that it's one of those days where I straddle the divide. It's a shock. Not unpleasant, but unexpected. My face is smooth, but I have not redefined the shadows or taken time to pluck the errant hair. It's the kind of look I used to go out on the street with, but only when I was prepared for stirring things up. I forgot I hadn't gotten around to deciding whether I'd go out.

That's why the cosmetics woman was so odd. Catching on in hindsight flusters me. The sudden urge to put myself together feels suspect. Like I'm trying to hide.

Back when I lived in the city, I liked to make it clear I wasn't all one thing or another. This upset people. Not just the guys on the street who bristled and stared. But friends, too. They thought I was making it harder for everyone. Meaning everyone who was working very hard at being one or the other. It's strange to doubt myself now, to feel that same hot flush of recrimination that shot through me sometimes back then. Strange to be surprised by a part of myself I did not think I had forgotten. I want to reach back to the young me and extend a cool hand. Give her a moment's rest.

I line my eyes in kohl as thick as Cleopatra's. I like my eyes, large and brown, like a deer's with no intention of bolting. Since I've been back in the city, sometimes I can feel some guy watching me. If we're standing at the curb, maybe waiting for a light to change, I turn and glance back. I take my time, look away and don't smile. Then I'll look back and hold his gaze with these soft, bold eyes. The look, real and purely feminine, assures him. Saves his face. And mine.

I brush my hair, throw on a simple linen dress that drapes well on my large frame, and tie a silk scarf around my neck. Alexandra at her cool best. I head back to my room, thinking I'll call Mary. It's been a while and it would be nice to hear a voice from home.

The guest room is the only room without many windows. There are three wide, short ones that span the top of the wall behind the bed where the light is filtered by jacaranda. Those frilly, southern fronds waving at the glass makes it feel like it's up in the trees. A sweet hideaway.

I call, but Mary doesn't answer. She'd be at school. I've lost track of time. Not unusual for me. But today it makes me feel awkward, restless.

I'm all dressed, ready for something, and I've been meaning to take Eleanor out while I'm here. Has to be lunch, though. That's the only elegant meal I can afford. Just another way to thank her.

On the way, the taxi driver flirts with me. He's a nice looking man. Not my type. I don't mind. Middle-aged and fit, elegant bones, swarthy and distinguished. At home, I never flirt. Everyone knows each other. The smallest innuendo could make a mess of things.

Eleanor is agitated when I get there. She looks a little rumpled and confused. She blushes and, for a moment, I think she's going to send me away. She doesn't like surprises, but she pulls herself together, and we head out to a French bistro in Brentwood that she knows. An intimate hole-in-the-wall where all the stars hang out.

We sit in the terraced brick courtyard under a white umbrella, and she orders a glass of Shiraz and Ahi with wild greens. I have the house salad and mineral water. She sits back in her chair and gazes at me. "You look glowing today. Did you do something with your hair?"

I'm about to tell her about the free make-up and the strange little woman, but I hold back. She might not want me making myself so much at home. I just smile in a mysterious way and thank her.

"You look great, Alexandra. Really. Have you ever thought about a little dermal abrasion to give your skin that soft look all the time?"

"You're not at work. Knock it off, El." She is keyed up today. Something's got her off her game, and she's struggling it get it back.

She laughs, apologizes, and then tracks someone entering the gates behind me.

"I don't normally do this. But Hoffman just came in. Don't look. I'll watch where he goes and let you know."

She is teasing me, and at the same time making fun of herself, Los Angeles, and all of it. I like seeing her like this, a little bedraggled from work, caught off guard, and loosened by wine.

"Do you like Hoffman?" she asks.

"Who doesn't?" I sort of doubt he's even here, but I let her have her game.

She takes a bite of her salad and drains her wineglass. When the waitress passes, she raises her glass.

"Do you like men or women?" She looks up from her greens, "I mean, what's your preference?"

I laugh, choking back the fizzing water. "I haven't . . . . I don't anymore. I'm celibate. It was a choice I made a long while back."

"Really?!" She stabs a pink slice of fish with her fork and examines it intently. "Why?"

"It just happened."

She leans back and takes a sip from the new glass, "We should get an order of the cheese and fruit. Organic goat cheese and figs. It's amazing."

"Of course. Whatever you'd like."

"What the hell, I have another hour, eh?" Trying to make the best of it. "So, then back before, was it men or women or both?"

"Men. Once I got old enough to know what I wanted."

"And now? You don't miss it?"

"No. You do." An easy deflection. When she gets too close, it just takes a slight flick of the wrist to get her back talking about herself. This way I can watch, try to figure out what's eating her.

"Incredibly. Sometimes I want to call Clarissa up and say, 'I know we're done as a couple, but we had some really great sex.' I want to remind her of that. I want to ask her if maybe we could just go on with that part, once in a while, you know?" Her face is bright and her eyes are glassy.

"I thought Clarissa was with someone else."

"She is. It's just that we knew how to make it work, physically. Right up until the end. It's so complicated with anyone else. More than I want to deal with."

"And sleeping with Clarissa is simple?"

"Why not?" She shrugs. "I asked her once. She said no." Her disappointment is strained. I suspect her mind is elsewhere. That she's talking about something other than Clarissa. Poor Clarissa. Even when Eleanor has her sights on something no one else can see, she is irresistibly magnetic— a galvanizing force. I can only imagine the mess of managing her when sexual tension is in the mix.

The waitress brings a plate with a wedge of white cheese, four plump figs, red grapes, and a squat jar of honey with a wooden drizzle. When she leaves, I say, "You just go for what you want, don't you?"

"Everyone does. I'm just more direct than most."

Eleanor can get away with it. She sits, elbows on the table, head propped up in her hands, white on white knit top and pants. Only she could sit so casually in something so immaculate and make out like it was everyday. It all works for her. Stunningly petite, a hard driving aggressiveness, it all lines up perfectly alongside her clean beauty. I watch her sometimes, seeing if I could mimic her moves, the way her presence commands attention, intensifies her femininity rather than detracting from it.

She puts two figs on her plate. "I can't resist these things. If I hadn't had a glass and a half of wine already, I'd get the tawny port." She leans across the table, "I have friends I could fix you up with. That's why I asked."

"Male or female?"

"I thought you could go either way. But celibate? That never occurred to me."

"It's uncomplicated. You should try it."

"If it was the right man, though, you would, right?" She leans in, savoring a bite of fig.

"I lost interest when I started hormones. My body was changing and just wasn't in a place to be that open. Then I just got used to it." I don't mind telling Eleanor these things. I've told her pretty much everything she's wanted to know in recent weeks. Things about my past, my body, why I went to the desert, and how the city feels both familiar and aloof. I just wish she would level with me, too.

"But maybe when you transition fully. I mean, who knows? Could be men, women, who knows, right?"

"Transition to what?"

"I'm sorry. I just thought . . ."

"I am who I am, El. This is it."

She nods and looks down at her plate.

Usually I'm not so blunt. It's better when I can handle stuff like this with humor. But today I don't. Sometimes I just can't.

I could shift the spotlight back to her. A moment ago, she had me curious, but I don't think I want to know anything more about Eleanor just now. We finish eating without saying much.

I pay the bill and take a bus back that stops a few miles short of the house. I can use the walk.

For a while, I think about Eleanor. It always surprises me how other people live. Not that they never have to think about their own gender, but that they never think of gender as anything but fixed. Eleanor sees me as not yet fixed. Amorphous. The outline of me is never out of the viewfinder, always in the crosshairs. Imagined and re-imagined, my image shifts inside her mind. I suspect this is why she is drawn to me.

I get off the bus and take the neighborhood in up close. The architecture ranges from Cape Cod to Frank Lloyd Wright. Groomed lawns spill from beneath freshly painted porches. Lush, tumbled gardens, rich with bougainvillea and passion flower climbing up villa walls. A private vineyard stretches up the hillside.

It's okay to stare at houses as I go by, even if I can see inside, because there's no one in them. I am drawn into the vacant stares of their windows. I move from one to the next, imagining where I'd live if I had the choice. Abandoned repose. As I pass, I dream that I slip inside each one, live a life, move on.

There was a time in L.A. when I imagined living like the wealthy men who sometimes brought me home. I'd dream about finding someone who had everything and wanted me to share it just because of who I was.

When all that broke apart, I made my way to the desert town. Cheap enough that I could live on the money from my uncle's estate. I made the decision to leave the city the same day the lawyer called. I threw the few things I owned in a bag and left. I would never have to work if I was careful. Never be something I wasn't for the sake of money or love.

I knew friends who worked the streets, got into the drug scene, disappeared. I settled in, out by the lake.

Maybe that's why the memory of Olivia keeps stirring in me. She reminds me of breaking away. Everything is different afterwards, and you can't go back.

I keep walking, pausing to look up driveways, imagining calling places like these home. Usually I take a taxi up and don't get to linger and take it all in. As the hill gets steeper, the houses more spread out, more grand and impermeable, I start to miss Mary. I start to miss my double-wide, even the smell of the lake. When I finally turn up Eleanor's drive, I am relieved. The white ranch house with its detached garage and vine-covered breezeway seem modest now. I open the door and drop the keys into the blue, ceramic bowl. I slip off my shoes and cool my swollen feet on the tiles. The place is huge with quiet.

When Eleanor sets me up with her charge cards, a rental car, and carte blanche on the new room, I waver. She is trying to buy me. I'm cautious, but it can be done. Though the intent must be sincere. So much is layered on top, it's hard to tell.

Maybe Eleanor just needs the room finished so she can move on, even if she hates it when it's done. She's been intense lately, even more than usual. Kind of off-key. I don't kid myself that the job will satisfy her. But I'm tempted anyway. That's the way the city is. Immersed in the flow of money, little pieces of yourself get worn away in the current. They don't seem like much at first. But they add up. The ride's got to be worth it; I think this one might be.

Each day rolls out Italian calf leather soft as flesh, hand-painted French silk, crisply woven Portuguese cotton. Designers are reserved but eager. They look me over and calculate how to please. I go through furniture row on La Brea. Every store. Make them wait on me. Men flirt, and sometimes, when I give them the slightest dash of male, women. I don't buy a thing. But I dress as if I might. And that, too, is a pleasure I'd almost forgotten.

Objects made by hand become my obsession. The finest materials worked by someone devoted to their artistry: cutting stone, dying wool, etching glass, bending iron. Hand hewn surfaces. Each piece unique, expressing the character of the material from which it was made. It is intoxicating. Completely absorbing. I become immune to the shock of price tags. Then I stop asking about price all together. The mouth of the beast yawns, and I look in, standing on his wet velvet tongue.

Usually I don't get so caught up in things. I don't buy a lot of stuff. But I know exactly what I would buy if I did. What kind of car or table lamp or the exact shade of white for a new cotton blouse. It's like I look at things, at physical objects, and they fall easily to one side or the other—yes or no. It's an instinctual equation of beauty, value, and necessity. The answer is always clean and irrefutable in my mind. That's why I like Eleanor's place. It's filled with things that all fall onto the yes side.

I bring home samples and survey them alone in the bare room, judging whether they can stand on their own. I settle on cool, minimalist lines with a nod to the phallic thrusts of art deco. Eleanor comes home each night. I parade new possibilities in front of her. She remains amused and detached, barely here at all.

I start looking for things that will wake her up, split the iris of her eye. If nothing else, things to make her laugh. But she is distracted. Everyday she goes to work early and comes home late. I take in her dry cleaning. Make her bed. Little things. She doesn't notice. She looks tired. Red around the eyes. One day I find a blown glass sculpture, flowing magenta petals splayed wide, revealing an interior so deep I can stick my entire arm inside. I bring it home on spec.

"Don't you think it's a little . . ." She sits at the edge of the ice blue chaise, the only thing in the room that's paid for. Both her feet rest on the floor, and her hands are folded neatly in her lap. She looks thin, almost gaunt, in the sheer silk tank and matching white pants.

"Thought it might cheer you up."

She rolls her eyes. "I hope you have the receipt."

"It was on sale. What's wrong? Don't you like it?"

"Is this a joke?"

"You'd think. But you're not laughing."

"It's been a day."

I sit across from her and wait for her to say more.

"I have this client. What she wants, I don't know."

She tugs her top down over her hips.

"Starting to second guess yourself?"

"No. That's not it."

She stands and runs her hands up and down her arms, calming goose bumps although the evening's warm.

"This one wants something different."

"How do you mean?"

"I mean, more than just the usual youth and beauty thing. Although, if I do the work, she will be beautiful."

"Newsworthy beautiful?"

"Maybe, but she seems very attached. Maybe a little too vulnerable."

"Too vulnerable? You're worried. That seems reason enough not to work on her, right?" I say this, but it's not the client's frame of mind I'm worried about.

"I could be wrong. The work could really mean something to her, really change her life in a way you don't see very often. Plus, what she wants, it would be a challenge."

"Not worth the risk though."

She nods, shrugs, and then stands abruptly, "I'll get the drinks."

Back with two glasses of gin and tonic fizzing on ice, she pauses in the doorway, then comes over and hands me one, "Something smells funny in here. Can you smell it?"

"It's hot and it's trash day." I take a sip. Heavy on the gin. "I think that's the first thing you've noticed about the room."

"Don't be ridiculous. We're in here every night."

"Exactly. And that's the first thing you've pointed out on your own. If you hate it, just say. It can all be undone."

"Of course not. Don't be so dramatic," she snaps, but there's no bite to her words.

I take the glass sculpture back the next day. At the gallery in Ocean Park, I wait for the salesperson to finish taking an order for blown glass shades—a custom chandelier. The buyer is sharply dressed in a dark gray cotton blazer, white oxford shirt, and khakis. He cuts a nice figure. Lately, I've been remembering how charged the city's anonymity can be. I'm checking the drape of crisp, ironed khaki over his round, toned ass when he turns away from the counter and stops in front of me, face to face.

"Alexandra?"

I look at him. He's wolf-eyed with feline poise, smiling a secret smile. Familiar from a long time back.

"Steven?"

"My God!" He reaches out to embrace me. "How long has it been!"

We go to the Rose Café for coffee. I can't get over the transformation. He was just a young punk, smart as a whip, living on the street, getting us hormones. Now he's all grown up. Blue-eyed, black-haired gorgeous.

"I went to law school, UCLA. Never could have done it without Isabel. Are you in town long? You should meet her. God! You should come up to our place in Goleta, we've got a little ranch. Isabel's made it our bohemian escape. We go there on weekends. Sometimes she spends the week, painting, writing."

"Sounds wonderful."

"What kind of place you got down there in the desert?"

"Just my own little hideaway."

"I thought I'd never see you back, when your uncle died." He adds the last tentatively. I left quietly. Never talked to anyone.

"Well, things change."

"Yeah, they do." He laughs and a bright, wide smile lights up his face. "You look so great. So happy."

Dressed for driving deals with designers. But Steven is radiant, and I suspect he shines a complementary light on everything he sees. "I do okay," I say.

"Don't you miss the city?"

"It's another life. Strange being back. Like being in the past, but not. Everything's a little different."

"I know that feeling," he says. I watch him. He hasn't touched his coffee. "Not about the city, though."

He takes a long breath. "I don't know why I need to say this, but I do. I don't need your approval, but I need you to know. I had surgery eight years ago, GRS and some others."

I nod. Of all of us, Steven was the one most adamantly against surgery, not just for himself, but for all transsexuals.

"I just came to terms with something deeper in myself when I met Isabel. Everything changed, healed. The desire for physical change was suddenly like a force moving through me. Painful, honest. I couldn't ignore it." He laughs once. When I don't join him, his brows raise and he looks straight at me, "What seemed all wrong twenty years ago suddenly became the very thing that would make me more me. Isabel saw me through it. Every step. Made her own way from lesbian to straight or whatever. It was unbelievable, the way we changed, the way we came through it together."

"Well, it looks like you're living right, that's for sure," I say because it's true, but I feel the old Steven, the one I knew, fall away. Out of reach.

"Everything from before seems like a dream." He takes a tiny sip. "I have to ask, you never considered it?"

"I always knew I wouldn't. That never changed." I don't know what else to say. His story has shaken me. Not in a way I would have imagined.

"I don't know why it was different for me, but it was." He shrugs, "I'm not apologizing, just trying to explain."

"It doesn't matter why, does it? It was right for you. That's what matters. Asking why will just drive you crazy. It's the wrong question, the poison dart." I try to make my face warm to match what I am saying. It surprises me how sad I feel. Not because we made different choices, but because the line between those choices still seems so fixed. Even the two of us, old friends sitting face to face and wishing the best for each other, might not be able to reach across.

His eyes light up. "I just knew, the minute I saw you, I had to say something. Scary. I was afraid you wouldn't see, wouldn't get it. I lost a lot of friends."

In the old days, anyone who did what Steven's done would have been cut loose from the circle and talked about long afterwards. Selling out, conforming, grabbing the high rung of the gender hierarchy, and reaping all the benefits of acceptability. Now face to face with Steven, all that seems beside the point. His glow comes from something real. I shouldn't be surprised, but in the plain light of it, I am.

He takes a long draw on his coffee. "Damn," he shakes his head and smiles brightly, "I've missed you, girl. Why have you stayed away so long?" But the smile is forced. I remind him of the past. The one we both thought we'd left behind.

"The pavement, the buildings, everything rushing around without touching, without slowing down. I didn't really realize it until I got here. It's a shock to be back."

I think of Olivia and the feel of her small hand on my back. I miss the lake now, more than ever, and the way small moments are not crushed by the force of more.

His eyes darken.

"Have you been out to the old neighborhood?"

I shake my head. He looks at me tenderly. I want him to stop.

"It's different now. Upmarket." Then he brightens, "Hey, you should come out to the ranch. Isabel would have a cow. I've told her all kinds of crazy stories from those days. She'd love to meet you." We exchange numbers. I watch him go, hands in his pockets, whistling strong, pure tones, no tune.

When I get back, I take a long walk through the hills above Eleanor's place. Right on up to the ridge where I sit at the base of a boulder and stare over the canyon, out to the water shimmering in the bright afternoon haze, cool and a little breezy. Scrubby canyon oaks shake their silver leaves.

I think about how hard and glorious it was back then. We knew it wouldn't last. Eventually, we'd have to find ways to live that weren't at the edge of everything. I think about the day the lawyer called to tell me Uncle Oscar had left me something in his will. And how I promised myself that if I took the money, no matter what, I'd never hate myself the way my uncle did. I wasn't going to be like that. I'd take all the best of him and throw away the rest. It gave me strength, that decision. The biggest one I'd ever made. I didn't feel lucky. But I felt solid, like I knew my way out.

It seemed natural at the time, just moving on. We didn't stay in touch. Could I have stayed and made my way here like Steven did? Not by having surgery, but by sticking it out? Could we have found some way to keep the past from breaking off? I thought I'd never come back. Why did I? Because of some missing girl and a strange woman who came looking for her? What kind of sign was that to follow?

I sit there, crushing the fine dirt under the sole of my shoe and smelling damp drifting up from the canyon on hot, rising air.

I spend most evenings on my own, sitting out by the pool in the evening breeze. A young coyote dips by, and I set out dinner for him. He eyes me warily but steps to the edge of the patio and takes the food with three gulping jabs. Then he looks once more at me, turns, and zigzags up the dusky hill. I think about trying to catch him and bringing him back to the lake, where there's not so much city. But I know nothing of canine territories, whether I would be setting him down in someone else's and if he would be strong enough to fight. I take the dish back inside and wash up.

When I'm done, I steal another glance at the room. There's more to do, but it's coming together. Before long I'll be headed home. Strange to think of that. My place seems so far away, almost out of reach. This house has taken its hold. I'm not sure I'm ready to go.

The city keeps shaking old memories awake. Sometimes I catch myself thinking I'll stop by my uncle's old apartment, the white stucco and tropical courtyard, his door at the end of an open air landing fenced with thin iron rails. For a moment, I think he's still there, that he'll open the door and let me crash on his couch until something better comes along.

The memory of his drawn and narrow face, so elusive before, comes back sharply now. The sound of his voice, the smell of old smoke. In his apartment, a gauzy, yellowed curtain filters the day's bright light. I'm sitting across the room, knees tucked beneath my chin, picking at toenails so short the skin around balloons up pink and puffy.

"James, you want everything. That's your problem," my uncle says. I roll my eyes and shrug. He's got that look he sometimes gets, face lead still, eyes tiny and horribly intent. It's like looking at someone trapped in a block of ice, trying to signal to you that they're still alive. "You just want it all. The world doesn't work that way, my friend."

I don't say anything. He shakes his head, lets his cigar rest in the cut glass on the table. I'm glad he's put it down. His favorite Cuban. Sometimes I can hear a funny little wheezy sound in his chest when he takes a puff and it gives me the creeps. Most things about him do. He's old, almost fifty. I'm fifteen.

"Hey, how about you and me go up to the Crow's Nest—see who's around? If you put on something more grown up, I bet George'll let you in."

He hates my skinny T-shirts and cut-off shorts.

I hate the Crow's Nest—the smell of alcohol, the room thick with smoke, no windows, old faggots pissing their time away, everyone pretending to be jolly.

Uncle Oscar always says it like it's a new idea. It's Sunday. We always go on Sundays.

"Sure, whatever." I put on the slacks and striped polyester button-down he bought for me.

We get into his wide, yellow Cadillac. He picked it up used, years ago, but it's pristine. No smoking inside. Waxed and polished every week. Bi-annual tune-ups at the car's original dealer. I remember the look on his face—was it one day or every time? The light changes and his hands shift into drive, foot gently squeezing the accelerator. He gazes out across the canary-yellow sheen of the hood as if this was it. This was The Life.

Just this one day a week. A twenty-minute drive from one eroded place to another. That was the only time I saw him look that way. It made me angry and sad in a way I didn't like.

Even so, I can't keep from watching him. We sail down Culver Boulevard in the bright afternoon. His face flushed, eyes alight, his hands up high on the wheel.

I stare out at the pool for another moment, letting the memory settle. Someone is knocking at the front door. Soft at first, then louder as I move through the house. The cosmetics lady. I'd thought the evening breeze was cool, but her face is damp with heat, her smile withered. I step back and move to close the door.

"I hope I'm not disturbing you," she says, because she knows she is.

She's wearing that same coral jacket as last week, already a little worse for wear. Nothing a good dry cleaner couldn't fix. But it hasn't been, and she is still wearing it. I remember all the times when I've had to make a choice between how I'd like to be seen or how I'd like to see myself, and the things I needed just to make it through the week.

I invite her in, and we sit out back with two tall lemonades.

She perches high on her chair, gazing out at the hills. "So much space up here. Wild, almost."

"Yes, it's wonderful." I look through her catalog. She has her case in her lap. The chrome is quilted in a diamond pattern. Very sixties, very retro. Only hers is a little bedraggled, like maybe it's the real thing.

"It's not my house," I say. "I'm a guest, just staying for a while." I hope the confession will dissuade her from coming back. I feel sorry for her, but she puts me on edge.

"Oh?" Her voice is mild. Not surprised at all. "Where are you from? Out of town?"

I feel bad now. The freebees, the long trek up the hill.

"Down by Palm Desert. Summers down there can be unbearable."

"Is that right?" Her brows knit with concentration. "I don't get there much. Must be nice." She lays out three applicators and an array of eye shadows.

"I'm not from Palm Desert, proper. Just south of there. I have a place on the Salton Sea." She doesn't look at me. "I'm sorry. I should have told you. I won't be around to be a regular customer."

She finishes rooting around in her case. "There we go." Her smile is cool now. She crinkles her nose strangely, and says, "That's okay. Really."

"I'll buy today. A few things. If you want me to pay you for the samples, I will."

When she speaks, her voice is low and choked, and she stares into the pool, "Tell me something. You ever just get tired? I mean just plain tired of who you are and where you ended up? You ever just want to up and get away from everything?"

The water ripples, casting blobs of white across the pool floor.

"I guess." She's doing it again. Saying things that could mean anything but aren't innocuous. I glance at the clock, wishing Eleanor would come home.

"But you don't, do you. I mean, it's got to be pretty bad to pick up and clear out." Then she shrugs, blinks, and turns sanguine, "No, we have to stay and face our troubles. Head on. No matter how bad they seem. Don't you think?"

I don't answer. I see grass move way up on the ridge and wonder if the coyote is lurking. Listening.

She lifts her glass toward me, and I take it.

"If I could have some more?" Her cheeks are flushed and her smile is a little wasted and flat. Right now, it looks like something that belongs to her. I go into the kitchen and load her glass with extra ice. I don't know what she wants. I could send her away, but it is awkward.

Back outside, she reaches for the glass and laughs a sharp hiccup. Then, her words cut loose: "I know someone who ran." She takes a long draw on the lemonade and swallows thickly. "Just about killed the one she left behind. Broke her up inside, real bad."

She smacks her lips and taps the base of her glass against the table a few times. Her legs are crossed lightly, and her right foot keeps bouncing, kicking at the air. "Real bad," she says again.

I don't say anything. Listening to her is like one of those games where a little wooden box is tilted and steel balls scatter over pegs. I keep waiting for one of those balls to land in a hole. Suddenly she starts to cry huge, gulping sobs. I stand, alarmed, then sit. Then I go inside for tissue. I think about locking the door behind me, but instead I go back out. She looks so pathetic huddled over the table.

She lifts her head, red-eyed, almost begging, "But what if someone could put back all the pieces, make it the way it should have been all along? I think that would be a start, maybe make the way forward more clear."

"I'm not really following you," I say. I sit next to her. We stare out at the hills for awhile, but I keep stealing glances at her.

Then she says, "Just think about it, right? A new start. The way it should have been but wasn't. That would be like a miracle, don't you think?"

She sniffles, blows her nose, and turns to look at me, "So who's your friend?"

"What friend?" I start calculating how much stuff I can afford to buy, try to guess how much will get her to snap back into business mode.

"The one you're visiting, who lives here." She watches me plainly.

"She's just someone I know."

"Nice place for a single woman."

I am relieved to talk about something else, but I don't want to say much. "She's a doctor, a plastic surgeon."

"Ah, now there's a job. She must get all kinds."

She keeps jiggling her knee, and it makes me think of Olivia out by the shore in the meager light of her fire, and how she said her mother was broken up inside. She even looks a little like the girl. Darker around the eyes than I noticed when we first met. Maybe that's what's confusing me.

I'm adding up the numbers, but they aren't coming out right because I want to ask when her daughter left, how old she was, and if she's heard anything from her. But her words hang between us, fragile and sore, and I don't want to make them more of a mess than they are. It can't be, I tell myself. There are thousands of runaways in a city like L.A. And I'm not even sure that's what Bunny was talking about.

The rules out in the desert do not apply here. Back home, when I suspect one thing is connected to another, I am always correct. Everything is laid bare and dependent. Here, my senses are swamped and my imagination must be running rampant.

"Seems like the place is big enough already for one. Why's she adding on?"

"The addition is just one room. She's had it redone a few times and still isn't happy with it. I'm trying to help her out. That's why I'm here."

Her brows raise. "Can I see?"

"I don't think that's a good idea." I need to find a gracious way to get her to go.

"What size are you?" I ask as I hold the pen and form out to her. "I can't pay you for the samples if I order all this, but I have a jacket I got on sale and it's all wrong for me. I bet it would fit you. Interested?"

She looks down at her jacket and then back at me.

"Final sale. I'll just give it away if you don't want it."

She shrugs, her face guarded but curious.

I go into the house and slip into Eleanor's room. She has a ton of clothes. None of which fit me. Inside her walk-in closet are rows and rows of things hanging neatly wrapped in dry cleaning bags. Pinks and whites and buttery yellows all pressed to a sheen. Back against the far wall, way back behind the black cocktail dresses and cropped dinner jackets, is a soft blue blazer in an Italian linen blend.

I come out with the jacket and some cash.

She folds the bills inside my order and then looks the jacket over.

"It's nice. Way too small for you, though."

"I grabbed the wrong one off the rack. My loss. Try it on." She shrugs off the coral one and slides into Eleanor's. Not a perfect fit. Tight around the shoulders and upper arms. But not bad. "Come on."

I lead her over to the cabana at the pool's edge where she can take a look for herself.

"How much?"

"No, it's yours. Didn't cost hardly anything."

"Why?" She glances at me in the mirror and then back at herself.

"Just because. I'm sorry I can't buy more after your coming all this way."

She nods, "That's nice. You're good to people. People you don't even know." She turns from side to side so that she can see herself from different angles.

I fold the collar of the jacket neatly around the back of her neck. In the mirror, my smile looks a little lopsided.

"It's a balance. Good to strangers, then not always so nice to friends."

"Guess I better stay a stranger, then."

We laugh, her smile timid and short-lived.

She leaves, and I go back outside. I see the coyote standing a little way up the hill, looking down at the house and sniffing the air.

The next Tuesday, I remember to call Mary at the store.

"Hey there, stranger. I was going to call. They're almost done at your place."

"That's great." I imagine the Plexiglas shower, fresh linoleum, and new fixtures. The bathroom will feel brand new. The work was, of course, much more extensive once they got into it.

"So we haven't lost you to the glamour of the city?"

I think of Mary standing behind the counter at the store, her face fresh scrubbed and freckly. All of it feels far away, not just the distance. "Mary? Can you do me a favor?"

"Sure."

"Can you get someone out to give the place a clean before I get there? Must be a mess."

"It's not bad. The workmen did a good job picking up."

"Still, it would be nice to come home to a clean house, you know?" I think about the way the towels in the bath smell a little like rotten eggs no matter how often they get washed, the odor sticking to me every time I dry.

"I'll ask Maria. Juanito fell and broke his tooth last week. She'd be grateful for a little extra."

I think about Maria moving through the house, wiping the dust from the table, mopping the floor, her boys playing out in the patio or on the living room floor. She relocated from the battered women's shelter in San Diego. I keep expecting her to have to steal away again, cut out in the dead of night. But maybe now, after a year, maybe she is safe. We all keep an eye out for her and her three boys.

I sit down that evening and make a plan. There is enough on the "yes list" to finish the room. If I set everything in motion, I can be out by the end of the week.

Asa

I don't like coming in here. It is full of secrets my daughter whispered into the ceramic ears of her kitten, the white rabbit, or the spaniel she called Lady. Moonlight slaps the low, single bed, the wooden chair, and the dresser where the animals cast long, strange shadows. Surfaces jump up out of the darkness in white, clean light. They shudder as if pulling free. It is dazzling. Like pooled electric current. For a moment, I think I see her standing by the window, and then she is gone.

She was my teacher's daughter. Just like my own baby would have been if my blood hadn't crested and flushed it away. The teacher's wife already had twins and a house and a husband. What did I have besides Olivia? I knew enough to expect that people won't always see things how they really are. Most are as scared as I was back then: a teenage girl, baby clamped to her chest, running toward dark. Can't see what's right in front of them.

I should leave her things alone. I found the doctor's card in jeans scrunched up at the back of her dresser drawer. Even if I put it back in the pocket and ram the jeans in again, I can't help thinking she'll know when she comes back. I don't stop looking, though. Even when it leads nowhere.

The card came from the place in Santa Monica. The clinic. I've been cleaning nights there for a couple years. Olivia used to come with me sometimes to read the magazines. Mostly I work in ugly places—cramped, stuffy offices in cement buildings with sour-smelling carpet. But this one is nice. They do face lifts, boob jobs, that sort of thing. Why would she have their card?

I remember black ice, a pink knitted hat with a bobble on top, the feeling of being whole again and scared because of it.

It's hard to know how cold it was that night. In my mind, it's the coldest ever in Victor, South Dakota. The ground was frozen and the air was too bitter to even think about when spring might come. I had lost my baby. Months too soon. Never moved or breathed or nothing. I would dream about her being found, all tiny and perfect like when I put her in the ground, but still alive. During the day, I felt like I was buried with her, stiff and permanent.

When I heard the teacher, father of my own baby, had a newborn, I couldn't help going to see. He lived in the part of town with split levels and shag carpets and wives like pumice, all pale and airy. His wife was pretty, too, and when I saw her I wondered why he ever bothered with me. I was pimply and gangly, barely female.

I knew he'd hired that fat girl from home economics to help out at the house, and I'd just seen her headed across town. She was on her way home, hunched up like she had cramps real bad. So I showed up at his door, like he'd called me up and sent me over. I asked the wife, "Didn't you get a call from him yet?" She let me in right away. No questions. No call to check or anything.

I spent all afternoon in his house, with the wife, the two toddlers, and the baby. The wife carried the baby on her long, slim hip, always moving like she had somewhere else she wanted to be. I ran after the kids to make the wife think

I knew what I was doing. But mostly, I watched the baby and wondered what it would be like to hold her.

On the phone, the wife chatted, sighing and laughing:

"What can you do?"

"Every one is a blessing."

"Even more so when it's not expected, I suppose."

"The Lord only gives what He knows one can bear."

I thought about my baby, tiny blue fingers curled in tight fists, pup-sized body balled up in a pillowcase. I wondered about that big, grown-up world I had not gotten into yet, whether the things that must be borne kept getting heavier and how anyone could stay so cool and full of air beneath that weight.

I thought about that all day. I wondered if it was true that the Lord gave people what they could bear and, if so, why he'd given me what he did and then took it away. My body was scraggly, all angle and bone. Did he think I couldn't take care of a baby? Wouldn't he have thought of that before he put the baby in me? Maybe it's humans that make the babies, and he just decides whether to put souls in them or not. When the Lord saw me carrying, barely showing, and no one else knowing or caring, if he gave a thought to me at all, it was probably that I was so used to being alone, more wouldn't matter.

But when a baby goes, it pulls the lining with it. Takes the cloth that held everything in place. After that, the loneliness is bigger than you knew it could be. It takes everything a person has, all the good and all the bad, to try and make sense of any of it.

When I passed the teacher's wife, pushing the baby in a carriage on the street, and she stopped me to ask whether I could come by next Thursday evening so that she might take the other children to an open house at school, the sense I made of it was that God was wrong. I thought maybe she had made up her mind, too. And we could set this right.

It was dark when I stepped into the neighborhood. Nine new split levels huddled on the edge of stiff, open fields. Bare saplings jutted up in the strip between sidewalk and street. I could see how nice that sidewalk would be come spring when the frost thawed and everything turned to mud. But I walked on the frozen dirt where there was grip, counting trees as I passed. I came to twenty-two just outside their walk.

The front door swung wide when I knocked, and the older kids spilled out in puffy, blue button-down coats and long wool scarves. The wife swept a kiss with her finger and put it on the baby's forehead, then hurried to show me the diapers, the bottles, the formula. She pulled on her coat and said they wouldn't be late.

The house held on to an ordinary evening. Chairs pulled up to the TV. Dishes in the sink. Clothes piled up on the dryer waiting to be folded: her slim legged canvas pants, boy's pajamas, his fraying briefs. Everything was cozy and smelling of soup and tangerines. Maybe everything would come back together. Not the way it was before, but back together in some way.

I sat for the longest time watching the baby sleep. Her face would clench up, then give way. Her eyebrows rose in the softest little arches. Blue veins in see-through skin. Was the baby dreaming? I wrapped her in the blanket and held her.

I knew that when the teacher came home and saw me sitting on his new, spring-green couch holding his child, he'd make sure I wasn't asked back. He was done with me. He'd started it all—asked me to stay after school because I hadn't done my homework right then told me some girls like to know what it feels like to be a woman and he thought maybe I was one of them. It felt good to be noticed, picked out of the crowd.

He promised I'd like it more when I got used to it, but I never did. I think he just wanted to be the first to try me out. He was done with me pretty quick once that was over. He never meant for it to go on, or for me to meet his family, or to come home and see me there, with his baby, sitting right where he and his nice, airy wife watched the evening news. It wouldn't take him long to make sure I wouldn't come back. Just mentioning I was from the foster home across town would be enough. If I said anything, he'd make sure I didn't have a leg to stand on. How long did I have until then? One hour, two at the most?

She would not remember it, but I wanted her to. I took her outside, just for a minute, away from the flat light of street.

She stirred but didn't cry about the cold. Then she opened her eyes, staring straight into the crusty fields stretching out into vaulted dark. When I craned around to see her face, she looked at me and smiled.

I left the door open. Behind us, the houses poured their feeble light down into the ground where my steps broke through the ice.

After I find that card in Olivia's pocket, the clinic seems different when I go to clean. Tonight, I should already be vacuuming the doctor's office. Getting along the ridges of the baseboard like they tell me to. In notes. Never in person. Instead of cleaning, I flick through the magazines, trying to see what Olivia was so interested in. But all I find are women so beautiful they've never had to worry a day of their lives. What was she looking at?

An easy night. I only have this one place. It has to be done just right, or they'll call the agency. But, still, it's just the seven rooms and one is behind a steel door with a thick little window where the doctor does her surgeries. I don't go in there.

I start vacuuming in the waiting room, put in an empty bag so I know I'll get every single little flake of dead skin or hair or chewed fingernail. First one direction all the way across and then at right angles, all the way back. And over-lapping, so you don't get lines in the carpet. The trick is to make it look like it's this way all the time, like no one had to work at it.

I empty the trash—paper espresso cups and subscription cards from magazines. I polish handprints from the arms of chairs. Dust the walls. Lift cushions and vacuum underneath. I wipe down the glass surfaces, the windows, the mirrors, the tabletops, the glass wall between waiting room and front office. It's critical that I don't leave a trace. Not a smudge. Not even the scent of cleaner. Especially scent. Nowadays people won't tolerate that sort of thing.

The night we left, South Dakota was cut deep with freeze. Running across those open fields, I was waiting for God to have his say, thumbs up or down. But there was only the stabbing cold and the feel of the baby against me. God was busy with other things. The two of us, moving fast and wily, we were just wilderness.

When we got to the highway, a bus was there all lit up by the side of the road. I stood just outside the circle of light and watched. The windows were dirty and steamed but I could see the blurry dark heads of a few passengers.

Then I saw a stocky man in a cap zipping up his pants behind the bus. He reached into his pocket, pulled out a flask, put it to his lips, and leaned back. Right then. That was our chance. I moved out from the dark, nodded once so he'd know I saw him, and stepped inside. Midway down the bus was a man with a trim mustache and a puffy, boy-ish face. He had his hands to his ears and stared down at his lap. Three seats back, a pockmarked kid was trying to get his hands inside his girlfriend's shirt. The guy with the moustache looked up in surprise and then out the window to figure out where I'd come from. I went straight to the back with the baby pressed close to me. Then he turned to frown at me. He frowned again for double measure, when he got off in Beulah, just over the Wyoming border.

The driver must've needed his job pretty bad because even when the APB came in, he kept his mouth shut. It was a long drive, all through the night and then some. I didn't know where we were going. She was wet and hungry. When she cried, my breasts wept and made stains on my shirt. But it had been too long. The milk was watery and, from the way she fussed, I guessed it was barely there at all.

We made our way down through Idaho and into Salt Lake City then across the Nevada desert and finally crossed the border into California. About the time I thought the ride would never end, we hit the wide-open farmland of the Central Valley. It was a lot like home, except there were also vineyards and groves of stunted, dark-skinned trees with frilly silver leaves. Olive trees, the driver said. Grapes and olives. Things that grow where it never gets cold. That's when I knew we had arrived. A new day, a new life. I looked at my baby and chose her new name, to mark the beginning.

When we stepped off that bus into morning, the air was warm and dry, the color of harvest fields back home. Even in February, it was like that in Bakersfield, California. People smiled at us as we passed them on the street on our way into town. We smiled back. Me and Olivia. Like that's the way it had always been.

I finish up cleaning later than usual. The sky gets light so early now. Daylight is the worst time. Exhausted, I won't sleep. I look around, take in the glow of the clinic's white shingles and the hanging pink blooms that look like bruises in the dim light. I think, Why not? Why the hell not? I go back to my car and throw on some clothes I've got in the trunk, nice pants and a blouse I've been meaning to take to the dry cleaners. They're a little wrinkled. But they look okay. I wait awhile, try to smooth out my clothes, watch the cars that pull into the lot to park, and the people who get out. When I can tell the clinic's good and busy, I go in.

A squat, square-faced receptionist looks up from her desk and motions me over. I tell her I don't have an appointment. "I can ask the Doctor but I think you'll have to come back another time," she says without smiling. "Fill these out." She passes me a clipboard already made up with papers.

I glance at the waiting room. Two others are lined up reading magazines. One's blonde. So wispy in her business slacks and thin white blouse, you'd think she'd blow away. The other is a red head with a boyish bob. She's in shorts and a tee. Muscular, sporty, no-nonsense. They are both very pretty and young.

I can't make sense of any of it. What are they doing here? I fill out the forms but I'm not going to hand them in. This was a mistake. I'm about to tell the receptionist never mind, but before I know it, she calls my name and leads me down the hall.

"Eleanor Renald." The doctor reaches one hand out and puts the other on the polished desk, leaving a handprint. She's lean and sleek, smaller than I imagined. Almost my size. But more polished.

She grips my hand and then gestures to the little couch. Too cushy for my liking. And too white. But there is nowhere else to go. Even when I sit up, my feet don't reach the floor. I keep falling in.

The doctor's confidence is as smooth as her good looks. Jet black hair pulled tightly from a heart-shaped face and smart, pale blue eyes. She is quick to scan my face and then, with a flick of her eyes, my chest, waist, and legs, as if I can be totaled up and fit in alongside all the rest.

"Nice place. Clean. Nice," I nod and look around me as if this is the first time and I am taking it in. On the carpet beneath her desk, there are marks where I was careless with the vacuum. In a corner, where the wall meets the ceiling, there is a single strand of cobweb caught in the morning light.

Her brow rises in neat little ripples.

She asks me what I'm here for. I don't answer. She taps the eraser of a pencil against the desk. Scuff marks polka dot the sheen. They just hover on the wide, dark surface, not quite joined to anything. It's that bright in here.

Finally, she turns the pencil on its point and looks at me with cool urgency, as if to say, "It's your choice. You can do what you want with your free twenty minutes." I feel it now, that pressure to say something. Only the pressure is coming from inside of me. I straighten up, check myself, and take note. She's good at this.

She doesn't know I am a mother, that I raised a child, that I am alone. She does not know anything about me at all. I want to ask her about Olivia. But I am just a client, stripped of everything outside this room. It doesn't feel good, but it's not bad either. I stall, "I just need a pick me up."

She nods. I wonder what she's got going on outside of here. A husband who is older but getting more distinguished with age, a big house with a pretty yard, two teenage girls who squeal over boyfriends and makeovers and college entrance exams.

She comes and lifts my face toward the light. Her palms against my chin are cool and silky. I close my eyes and see the outline of her shape in the afterglow of light. It's been a long time since my face was touched.

Her voice is smooth and calm: "Well, let's see what we can do, shall we?"

Once, when Olivia was young, we met this girl at the park. I could see right away there was something wrong with her. She sat huddled in red shorts and a pink jacket even though it was sunny out. She was a little older than Olivia, but she hummed and moved her toys around in patterns only she knew. Everyone stole looks at her. We were all trying hard not to, but we all kept looking. Olivia went right up to ask if she could play. The girl just ignored her, but Olivia kept talking as if it was a normal conversation. The more Olivia talked, the more the mother got this funny little look on her face that was almost a smile. The mother looked tired.

We hardly went to the park without me thinking some-one was watching us, first because Olivia was pretty, then because we didn't match. The fear would seep in down deep through the pores of my skin. People couldn't help notic-ing Olivia's dark silken hair and smoky eyes. How fresh and sweet she looked leaning in close to that little girl who hardly glanced at her. Maybe that's what Olivia liked about the girl. Maybe, even that young, she was getting tired of being watched.

Olivia told the girl where we lived, but she could never pronounce it right, which was a relief. No one needed to know our business. And then she reached out for one of the girl's toys, a green frog, I think. The mother leaned in like she was going to stop her, but held herself back because her little girl was finally looking at Olivia. Olivia smiled, and the girl just stared. Olivia started telling her about tadpoles and frogs.

She said, "Frogs breathe through their skin. They have to stay wet, or they'll die."

The little girl was blank-eyed, but her mother was nod-ding and smiling.

"That's right. Anna knows about that, don't you Anna? Animals that do that, what are they called?" I could see Olivia struggling not to answer. It was a very long time before Anna spoke. She looked up into the sky and scrunched her face, and we all waited, her mother nodding and Olivia's mouth hanging open in a silent "A."

Then Anna, still looking at the sky, said "Amphibians." She tucked her head down and moved her toys in strange, circular motions.

We all laughed because it felt good that she knew we were here, that she wasn't all alone. I edged closer and Anna's mother told me her name was Colleen and asked what was my little girl's name. Olivia started picking up more of Anna's toy animals, one by one, looking at each up close.

"She doesn't let just anyone do that." Colleen laughed. It was a tired little laugh, like she would rather just lie down on the bench than talk to me. "Your Olivia's special. Sure is pretty, too." Colleen was tall, overweight, and she had a hard time looking at anything but Anna.

"Thanks," I said. Because we were talking, the woman pushing her tow-headed boy on the swing thought she had license to watch outright. I wanted to look around to see if others were, too.

I tried to think of a normal question, "How old is yours?"

"Seven."

I nodded, knowing I had stepped right into the subject everyone who was watching was wondering how I'd avoid. She did not act seven.

"She's shy. But you should see her once she gets going." Colleen's face cracked wide, teeth as white as the sun. Younger than I first thought, maybe my age. "She's a regular encyclopedia!" Colleen looked at Olivia wistfully, then, without looking away said, "Anna is autistic. She has trouble interacting. But she likes Olivia. I can tell." Anna looked up again at the sky, her brow a deep rut.

"Frogs and toads. Salamanders. Not lizards," Anna blurted and then looked at Olivia flatly.

Not to be outdone, Olivia shrugged and said, "I guess." Her answer for anytime someone knew more.

Colleen smiled. She seemed nice enough. No reason why she ended up with a child like that. I thought about what that must be like. Did she wish she didn't have her? I would have.

I wanted to turn away, to grab Olivia up and go. But I couldn't.

Anna took the toys back from Olivia. Neither made a fuss. Anna set each one back exactly in the place it was before.

Colleen said, "They get along so well. Do you think maybe Olivia would like to come over and play sometime?"

Olivia looked at me and asked, "Can Anna come and play at our house?"

Anna's head cocked halfway like she was listening, but whether it was for my answer or to some bird, none of us knew. The woman by the swing stared. They were all waiting.

When I think back to it now, I try to remind myself that I was barely out of my own teens. I still bought girls' clothes. They were cheap, and I was thin and running hard inside. I think about that because I don't feel proud of that day.

Olivia wouldn't understand this part. She was beautiful, in that poised, thoughtful way, the kind of beauty nobody minds watching while they wait for an answer, the kind that makes the watchers curious about what you'll say, no matter what it is. They just want to know. Her beauty slowed things.

When you're ordinary like me, time rushes at you and makes your thoughts all jumbled. People watch you and imagine what they would have said instead of you. Before you even say a thing. Colleen stood and beamed, "Anna? Would you like that, honey? How about we visit Olivia at home?" She looked at me, "Maybe next Wednesday morning, a week from today?"

Anna started to hum.

"That means she's excited!" Colleen whispered loud enough that we could all hear. "Let me get your address and phone, and I'll call you later this week. Okay?"

I felt dizzy and stretched out inside. All I could do was nod. I wrote something on a piece of paper she had in her purse and gave it back.

When we got to the car, I still had a forced smile on my face. It was stuck there. Maybe it was what made Olivia think it would be a good time to ask. Or maybe she was just so excited she had to say it: "Mommy, can we stop on the way home and see if we can find those little animals like Anna had? Please?"

"You like those, huh?" My smile was real, now. Something only she could do.

"I want to get ones Anna doesn't have. So that we'll have more when she comes. Maybe we can get one she can take back with her." I could see the whole day in her voice: how she would answer the door when Anna came, show off her room, let Anna find the treasure, how they were already friends.

We stopped at four or five stores before we found them. She picked out the Persian kitten, the spaniel she called Lady, and for Anna, a bright red tree frog.

Wednesday came. She waited by the window in her white sweater with the crocheted yellow flowers and Mary Janes already too small for her feet. I made cupcakes with pink frosting and white cake. When it was ten o'clock, she could barely stay still. Even I started thinking they might show up.

Our house is hard to find, even if you know what you are looking for. It's down a long, dirt drive that runs behind houses fronting the street, and the mailboxes are at the bottom of the hill, all grouped together with no clue to which numbers belong to which houses. It is private and out-of-the-way. That's why we moved here.

So Olivia understood, as the first hour went by, why they were late. And then, later that morning, how they might have gotten lost and turned back home. She played all that day with Lady and the kitten, leaving the bright frog for Anna on her dresser.

She never knew what I had done, although she might have guessed from the way I bought up those animals. One at a time wouldn't do. Most were part of families—mother, father, and at least one baby. All kinds of animals: snowy owls, chestnut horses, lop-eared rabbits, and squat, mud-colored turtles. We didn't have money to spare, but instead of going to the park we went to the toy store, then back home. After a while she didn't ask about Anna anymore and the red frog joined the rest in endless hours of backyard play on the burnt summer grass.

I turn on all the lights now when I clean. I want to get it right. I look through the doctor's portfolios and see the work she does. Her office should be done carefully, too. I take my time, going over and over places that look clean, just to be sure. If I come back during the day, I do not want to find that I have missed something.

I stay all night to get it right. Almost twice as long as before. But I take breaks, too. Sometimes I just sit and read. On the shelf behind her desk, I find a notebook labeled "Testimonies":

> "Dr. Renald is an artist. I came to her when no one else could help. Little by little, we worked together after the accident. Today, I look in the mirror, and it's like it never happened. No one would ever know."

> "I struggled for years as an aspiring actress. Two visits to Dr. Renald and I got my first big break, a major Hollywood film. Sometimes, it takes more than talent. Dr. Renald gets that. She helped me achieve my greatest goals."

> "I was so scared, but Dr. Renald put me at ease right away. It's like she sees what's unique in each person and wants to make it shine."

> "Don't put off those little fixes you think no one notices but you. Stop procrastinating! Dr. Renald can help. Everyone you think doesn't notice does. But they'll only tell you afterwards."

It goes on and on for pages. A cache of quotes she must use for marketing. If she even needs to market anymore. Her calendar looks pretty full. I stop reading, close the book, dust its spine.

These people are crazy. If Olivia was here, we would look at the quotes together and laugh.

No, if she were here, I wouldn't show them to her. Why is it the Olivia I remember could sit here with me and laugh at these? No, not the real Olivia. She wouldn't laugh. But why did she have the doctor's card? Even the Olivia I thought I knew is disappearing.

When I get home, I can't sleep. So I spend all day making flyers with Olivia's photograph. Last I heard from the police, someone reported seeing her down south. Camping at the edge of what turned out to be the most god-awful lake called the Salton Sea. That was six months ago, way back when she first ran away.

I went out, put up notices, but her trail was cold. I used to put my own number on. But you can't believe the crackpots who call. Cruel bastards tell me they have her, what they've done to her, or plan to do, how she sounds when she's in pain. They get me listening up until some detail slips in that's wrong, and I can tell it's just another sick lie.

I put the Salton Sea on the new flyer, though, with information about calling the police. I make hundreds of copies, Olivia looking out from each. The next day I put them on every windshield, telephone pole, and unmonitored notice board I can find all the way up Santa Monica Boulevard into Westwood then back down Wilshire. I'm out all day, until every one of them is gone.

My eyes are closed. The marker's cool felt tip nudges the skin beneath my right cheek. The light is strong. From inside my lids look like red wool. Crooked circles drift across.

Took me two weeks to get up the nerve to schedule the surgery after that first appointment with the doctor. Then it was a month and a half of thinking I'd change my mind before the actual day.

It's crazy that I'm here. I can't afford it. Nothing I ever wanted, but I've been looking in the mirror a lot, trying to see what the doctor sees. She says I will look more youthful, but I don't think that's what I'm after. Lines have crept in around my eyes. Sharp, harsh lines. Sneaky little tracks to the place we are now.

She touches the pen to my jaw. She will take away the little droop. Give me a stronger line.

When the doctor stops, I stare up at the light, blinking the glare from my eyes. She is smiling, as cool and sure as her fingers.

"Okay?" I ask.

"I think we're ready." Her brow knits for a moment. "Any questions?" Already, she is turning away.

I say nothing.

The doctor turns back to see if I have heard.

I say something about how good it must feel to do the work she does. Then I ask, "Can I keep the pen?"

She tilts her head to examine me, then shrugs.

"Why not?"

I tuck it in my pocket. Something to bridge this moment and after.

When it is over, back at home I look in the mirror. I am still me. Puffy faced, but still the same round splotch of a nose, drab little mouth, and thin, brown hair that hangs all wrong even when it's just been cut. A relief? Not quite. Around my eyes, it's like crusty, rust-colored eyeliner was put on with a shaky hand. The lids are swollen and pale. I look like I have been pulled out of the ground.

Something that was hard inside wriggles. A new sensation. What is it? Something left over? Something that can't get out.

Babies look so small and fragile, but their force can crack stone.

I want to talk to the doctor. I'd like to know how it was with my skin peeled back. If I can hear her voice, I might remember how she held my face. I call her office, get the message machine and an emergency contact. I write it down then tell myself this is not the kind of emergency she means.

By the next week, the swelling is getting better. I stare in the mirror for a long time. Long enough that the person staring back at me starts looking like someone I don't know. It's then I notice it. The rim of one eye looks nicked. The right, lower lid droops, just slightly.

I bend close. The left eye looks fine, and it started out pretty much the same as the right. What the hell happened here? I keep staring in the mirror thinking that there must be some mistake. Now my face, never beautiful to start with, is lopsided. Just slightly. Just enough to make everything look off. Like I was in an accident long ago, and surgeons couldn't put me back together.

When Olivia was seven, she asked me tell her again about her daddy, the story of how we met on a beach in Mexico and how he told me in a language that wasn't Spanish that he and I had the chance to make something beautiful in that one night even though we would never see each other again.

She was in second grade and sharp as a tack. She had her own rules: on Tuesday and Thursday, she wore dresses or a blouse and skirt because she liked the way the skirts blew around her legs when she ran; and on Monday, Wednesday, and Friday she wore pants but no panties because cloth against cloth made her feel itchy and bunched up. That was how she was.

She was beginning to notice things. Like sometimes I said we met in Puerto Vallarta and other times I said Acapulco. Once I told a mother of her classmate that I'd always wanted to travel but had never been out of the country.

One night when she asked to hear the story for bedtime, we were still watching TV. The blue made her face look sad, but she was smiling. I thought about telling her the truth. I knew I could say it so that she would understand. I wanted to spill the poison, look into those eyes like porch doors with their screens blown wide, and tell her that she was not where she belonged but that she was where she was meant to be. Her body radiated heat.

When the TV went off, I carried her to bed. We were both quiet as I tucked her in and she settled back against her Wonder Woman pillowcase, the one we picked up at the second-hand store and she wouldn't sleep without. I sat beside her on the bed.

"Tell me the story of Daddy," like a song.

"We met in Mexico. He was dark and handsome, as handsome as you are pretty, as strange as you are sweet."

She held her arm out for me to nibble when I said 'sweet' and giggled like she always did.

"He spoke a language I didn't know, words I had never heard. I thought maybe I was dreaming."

"What did he sound like?" she asked. She always asked the same questions.

"Like water running underground," I said. She blinked slowly.

"How did you know what he was saying." Not a question. The start of something to be finished.

"I just did. Just like I knew you when you were born."

"Tell the rest. The rest." She scrunched down and pulled the covers around her neck, closing her eyes lightly so that I would know she was trying to sleep but still awake.

"When we danced, he moved so graceful. When he ate, he ate slow, like each taste was new. When he sang, his voice was soft and husky. When I cried because he had to go, he held me. His hands cradled me like a boat. I wanted to sail away in them."

Her eyes flew open, and she looked at me then shut them tightly. She whispered, "Where did he go, Mommy?"

"I don't know, honey. The same place he came from, I suppose." I could feel him then, that man I imagined as her father. He was as true as something that had really happened.

The words had become nice after so much telling again and again, but the story was getting worn. We needed something solid to shore it up. That night, she said to me: "Tell me about where he came from. Please? Please?"

Her words blew through me. That night, we built the land around a fairy tale.

"Where your daddy came from, the leaves are as big as ears on elephants, and muddy green, like the ocean when it's stormy out. When it rains there, it rains for days, non-stop, and streams turn into giant rivers that wipe out whole villages built from scrap paper, because the villagers always know their houses will probably float away someday. When it is sunny, it's sunny and hot for weeks. All the mud dries up and cracks so wide that cats jump in and chase the little frogs and bugs and mice, everything down in there looking to stay cool."

She did not open her eyes, but her face lit up so brightly, I went on.

"There is no winter or summer there, only spring, so the trees and brush are thick. Everyone carries long knives to make their way because paths can overgrow in one after-noon. This is the kind of place your daddy came from, and his daddy, and his daddy before."

I did not know what I would say next; the land opened up before each word, and I could see him standing there—a tall, honest, olive-skinned man with eyes like coals and hands like hammers. I could see him smiling at us both.

"He has such dark eyes, Mommy," she said, eyes still closed, "and the water is so blue."

I tried to give her a story that was as beautiful as she was. It was not real, but it was true. I wonder, did she go off to find him in that place? Her origins were magic. I tried to tell her this in a way she could understand, with color she could live inside.

Did she always believe it was true, both the country and the father? I may have given her something she loved but could never hold and know was real. I'd like to know what was the worst of what I did, which more poisonous: making up what's true or keeping it inside?

At the clinic, I march in past the waiting room with pretty ladies all wide-eyed and looking at me—I'm their scabby, puffy-faced nightmare. The receptionist is away from her desk, so I just go right in, down the hall, and through the doctor's door.

I stand over her desk, finger jammed up in her face. "I'm going to sue your ass." She is studying her files.

"I'm sure we can . . ."

All morning I've been spitting mad. I clean up after her every little scuff and smudge all night. The place looks spotless. Stunning in full light. And she can't get my face right?

"There's no we in this, not as in you and me. There's just me, and your ass. The ass I'm going to sue."

She stands and peers at me. She reaches for my face. "Hold still."

"Get your hands off!" I jerk back.

Jesus, she's got nerve.

"Hold still!"

"I just came to tell you." But there's nothing more that I haven't already said, so I clam up.

"I can see what you are talking about, but I want a closer look."

She pulls out a giant plastic coated magnifier. She's blurry and bigger on the other side. I see her eye, her nose. Her fingers, tiny by comparison, reach toward my face.

"The incision was a little jagged."

I've got her. Right there. Wish I'd brought a tape machine. Why the hell didn't I?

She holds the eye open and stares. "It can be fixed. There's no need . . ."

"Let go. My eye's getting all dried out. Let go!" But I'm sorry when she does let go. When she puts her hands on my face, everything gets clear and all lined up the right way.

Even the feeling that I'd like to throttle her. It's the way she touches, as if I'm something she can shuffle back into place.

"I'm sorry." She stands back but her face is serious and keeps scanning me.

"I bet the lids don't close right anymore. That's probably why I feel so friggin' dried out." I almost swear but stop myself. She really does look sorry.

"The lids meet fine. It's the appearance, not the function. We can fix it." She sits. Elbows down, her hands meet together at the fingertips. "It will be such a minor operation. Not like before. You will heal very quickly."

"Right. Like I'd go under the knife again with you?" I think about going to another surgeon's office, the intake, the waiting, the rigmarole, the cost. It's not like I even wanted this done in the first place. I just got carried away. She was so confident and all.

"I understand. Completely. Can I recommend a colleague?"

"You're going to pass me off? What is this!?"

"Naturally you're upset. It seems enormous, I understand. But, from here, it's quite hard to detect."

"With your head up your ass, I bet it is." I'm arguing now because I don't know what else to do, and I don't want to walk out. Not yet. I don't know what I expected once I said my piece. It only took about thirty seconds. I should have thought it through. I should have gone another night or two.

"Look, what can I do to help? You're here, and I'm listening. What do you need from me?" She folds one hand down over the other and leans back as if she is relaxed—has all the time in the world. I saw them lined up out there. She doesn't.

I want to storm out, but I can't. If I do, I don't think I'll be able to come back. Not during the daytime anyway. To make it worse, tears start gushing, and I try to talk through them, babbling like a snotty-nosed child. What an ass I am. A complete idiot. She just watches me smoothly and calmly, and the shame moves deeper.

"She left me. Gone," I blurt. I am still standing over her desk but all kind of huddled over now because I do not know whether to sit or leave or try to get angry again. I do not know what else to say. The doctor is silent for a moment. I cry some more, and she hands me tissues.

A mechanical chime strikes nine, and she says very gently, "Look, why don't you make an appointment out front? Tell Sandy I said to make time, whenever works for you. We can take care of this. No charge."

I keep on bawling all the way out through reception. People stare, but that doesn't stop me.

I cry all the way home. My insides are huge and reckless. When I get there, I lie down and fall asleep like the dead, right up until I have to go to work.

When I go back to the clinic, it's different again. It's me I'm cleaning out of her office. I am floaty and calm. Fluffing my shape out of her pillows. Polishing the magnifying glass where she touched it looking through at me. I take my time, clean up everything, making it nice again. She'll fix my eye. Soon. For free. It will have to be free. Because I put the first surgery on my credit card and can't keep up with the payments. I don't know when they'll cut me off.

She says I'll look like a younger me. A younger me, is that good? She seems to think so.

When she touches me it's like she's sounding out what's underneath. I don't know what she hears. A little silver hammer on tin. The sound, the shape of me, it all goes into her light blue eyes and pools up.

I don't find anything anywhere in her office about unsatisfied customers, lawsuits, or malpractice attorneys. I can't find the keys to the file room, so that's off limits. But if she were not completely competent, I'd find some clue.

I find out a lot of other things, though: what music she likes, what she takes to dull pain, how often she sees a therapist. And some things make me curious: a news article about her that mentions a break-up. A divorce attorney's number on speed dial. Turns out, all my ideas about who the doctor is outside of here were wrong. Her private life is not so private. Pity, that. In the trash can, a torn up draft of a settlement plan from a woman named Clarissa.

Mostly, though, it's just article after article about satisfied customers, her accomplishments, lectures she's given. Each time I read a little more. I come across an interview in a women's magazine with the doctor and two of her patients. Mother and daughter. R's the reporter, S and T are the patients, and E for Eleanor Renald:

R: "It's not unusual these days for mother and daughter to team up for surgery. But you both have the spotlight on you. What went into making the choice?"

S: "Well, it was just something we wanted to do together, you know? I mean, we've always had things we like to do: shopping, spa, girls' night out. Why not go through it together so that you can have support? Make it an experience. Something more than just surgery."

T: "I wanted breast augmentation, and Mom wanted her first lift. We were both a little nervous. You are, everyone is the first time."

R: "So you wanted to be there for each other?"

S: "We wanted it to be a thing we shared. A new step for both of us. Taking it side by side means something."

R: "Dr. Renald, is this a good way for women to take their first step into cosmetic surgery?"

E: "Let me just say that, in this kind of case, it's more than just having good support. There is so much I can tell from working on mother and daughter. I have, right in front of me, examples of how one looked younger and how the other will age. It is easier to highlight the beauty but stay true to their essential look when I have variations on the theme to study."

R: "That's a point. But what about the father? How does he figure in?"

E: "It would be ideal to have all three. Maybe that will happen. But it hasn't yet, not for me."

R: "So, you make them look more like each other?"

T: "Don't you wish, Mom?"

S: "I'll never look twenty again! But just look at me, what good care can accomplish! Why would I want to look twenty?"

E: "And that's not the goal. They each have their own beauty. The plan of how to actualize its fullest potential is different for both. Partly because they are at different phases in their lives. But mostly because they are unique and this must be preserved. People come to me all the time and want the newest nose or chin or whatever is in fashion. I try to discourage this."

R: "But you just said you use one as the model for the other so . . ."

E: "Only to understand the building blocks. What they were born with. What parts of their heritage they will want to maintain. Especially when the bond is so close, as in this case, they are so close to each other. It would be a shame to destroy that physical link. It's important, who we come from. It makes us who we are."

This one hooks me. I read it again and again. At first I think I'm just angry because this mother and daughter take so much for granted. They make jokes about each other, like it's something they just get to have. I brood on that a little. They've got money. Bet it's easy being a mom when you can go shopping and get facials together. I read through again more slowly and then I realize what I'm feeling isn't anger. It's more of that tight buzzing that comes just when you're about to know something important. It's not in what the mother and daughter say, it's in the part from the doctor. How she wants to keep from wrecking the link, the way they look alike. If they didn't, would she nudge each of them that way? Would she make up little parts of the link if it wasn't strong? The doctor really cares about getting those two women right. It means something to her. That makes me more curious.

The hours slip by. I go through every notebook in her office, but it's not enough. I only know bits and pieces. I'm not done cleaning by the time I have to leave. I have to get out before anyone shows up, but I'll drop by on my night off, just to make sure the place is up to snuff.

After the doctor's done with the free fix, I'm taken to a private room to rest. A young voice, singing high and pure, drifts out from speakers in the ceiling. A full carafe of water, a clean glass, and a small vase of flowers sits on the table next to the bed. My head is quiet, all clean and orderly, just like the little recovery room. It's nice.

When I get up, I want to see her again, to tell her thanks, but she's working.

So I wait, dozing in my car, but when she comes out, I just watch her get in and pull away. Without thinking why, I slip into traffic behind her.

I thought she would head west, toward the sea, and maybe a little north, where all the high-end houses cling to the cliffs. But she is going east, inland, and moving fast. As we hit the freeway, the air gets hard. I roll my window up.

More interesting than I thought. Maybe she lives over the mountains, where houses are cheap. Maybe she really did lose a chunk when that woman left her. That would be a laugh—me living west of the mountains, while she has to schlep her way east everyday. Not a mean laugh, just an ironic one. She has enough on her plate without me threatening to sue.

I think about her holding my face in her hands. She's telling me everything will turn out beautifully.

She has a nice car. One of those black, convertible jobs with the sleek lines. It suits her. I can barely keep up. She moves over cracks in the highway like ripples, but my car hits them and jolts.

My head begins to throb. I search my junked-up glove box for the pills I got after surgery. She was right, it was a quick fix. But they had to numb me up. My car's a mess. What the hell did I do with them? Flyers of Olivia. City maps so old they're in pieces. Mop heads someone threw out even though they still had use. And that's just the front seat.

When I look up again, I think I may have lost her. It's getting dark, and all the running lights look the same. Maybe I should head back.

One by one, cars ease off the highway and new ones climb on. Just when I'm about to give up, way up ahead is a flash, squat and bright. Her turn signal. We're somewhere called Diamond Bar.

She pulls off the highway, and I find her at a McDonald's. Jesus. Mickey D's? I slip in behind to hear her order a Big Mac and fries. Even I don't eat like that anymore. I think about her peeling back the paper and stuffing the burger between her perfect, white teeth, sauce dripping on her nice blouse, and I think, what the hell, and order one too. I get the same thing she does except the Diet Coke. Those artificial sweeteners give you cancer. I get the lemonade instead.

My face feels swollen, raw around my eye. I reach into my bag and scramble around. The light here is bright and I spot the little orange bottle at the bottom. I let her pull forward, careful not to lag so far back that the cars behind start honking. I want to pull out of the line and into the dark, but I need that lemonade to wash these down.

When I get to the window, I grab the drink and swig down three pills. I can't remember if I should take two or four and my eyes are so bleary I can't read the label. Then I have to gun it because she is heading right back for the highway.

She keeps heading east. She can't be going home. I am tired, but I can't give up now. My car hits a bump in the road, one I didn't see in her glide, and pain jabs like a poker through my skull. The lights of houses thin out. The night sky clenches tight as a fist. The highway is straight and flat and dark. Around us, the desert moves in. I think maybe she is heading for Palm Springs, an exclusive spa with tropical plants lit up from spotlights in a thick carpet of turf. I would like to see that. But she passes the exit and keeps going.

My head starts feeling better. All of me is getting light and relaxed, drifting. Not so much traffic now. Her car is easy to track. Taillights like bright little beacons. I just keep heading for them. Then signs above say a new thing. Dreamlike now: the clean, white letters on a green background. The Salton Sea. First five miles and then three and then Next Exit and I think I must be sleeping in the quiet room after surgery, with a clean floor and flat white walls. It's like I imagine the sound of the turn signal, and the feel of the engine easing, and then, a few miles off the highway, the smell. God, the smell. No dream. Like forgotten fish tanks and eggs gone bad.

Like the backwash of something awful swilling behind you.

Her car sweeps over the gravel road. Mine tumbles behind. If only she would turn back. I want to honk, grab her attention, slam my bumper into hers. My skin pricks. Deeper than numb. She pulls into a wide, unlit, dirt drive that empties into boat launch parking. Police cars line the edge of the dark lot and bright lights dot a spot way up the shore. An officer hails her with his flashlight, talks to her, then turns her away.

I move in close behind, turning with her, but the cop puts his hand on my hood and leans into the crack of my window making the signal to roll it down.

His eyes are blank, and he looks like he's going to tell me to keep moving. But then he bends closer and peers at me. "Don't I know you?" he asks, leaning in so far I can smell the peppermint on his breath.

It's dark, but in the light of my car, I see he's the vacant-looking one that listened and grunted, feet up on the desk, hands resting on his round belly, when I came out months ago to find Olivia.

The doctor has pulled up to a closed shop at the back of the lot. A few shadowy figures mill around the dark porch and two sit on a front bench, staring out at the commotion and the lights on the water up the shore.

"I'll move on, sir." I fix my gaze at my knuckles on the steering wheel. He doesn't take his hands off the window. Peppermint and the smell of dead goldfish floating in a green tank.

"You're the runaway's mother, right?"

His fat, pink lips pucker beneath a thick mustache.

"We left you a message. Didn't mean to alarm you. We thought . . ."

"Olivia?"

"It's not her. We thought it might be. It's not her." He reaches down to lay his hand on the window's frame. I jerk away.

My head rings loud and high.

"Olivia?"

"We left you a message. A body of a girl was found. We thought it might be your daughter. But it's not. It was an OD from a party in Palm Desert. Jackasses freaked out and dumped her here. I'm sorry for the confusion, ma'am. We called again when we knew, but we must have just missed you."

I can't look at him. He is talking about some other girl, some other mother's child, some mother who will be blindsided, not staring ahead toward disaster like me. I cannot look at his eyes soaking up the dim light and his fat, damp lips.

I turn the car away from the officer, nailing the storefront with the beam of my lights. He strides fast alongside me so I stop again.

I stare ahead, wondering why the doctor brought me here. How she knew when I didn't. Why her card was in Olivia's pocket. She looks out at me, blinking, blinded.

She is talking to a tall man in the shadows. Then she leans toward him but he does not reach for her. She looks so small beside him. He is shaking his head, bowing slightly. All this is sifting in and around as the officer is saying something that I'm not listening to. Everything outside of me is soft and almost kind—the sound of his words and the sight of the doctor leaning in as if for an embrace. It is all patterned, smooth, and clean. I want to lie down.

The officer is quiet now. I turn a scowl on him, "Well, you got me all the way the hell out here. How about a hotel room?" I am dizzy, but I have enough sense to know it is best to come off confident. Irritation is even better, if you can get away with it. Knocks them off guard so that they stop thinking. I avoid police. But when Olivia left, I had to learn how to handle them. When they start thinking, you'd think that would be good. But it's always when the trouble starts.

I keep watching the doctor with the man. He steps out into the full beam to put his arm around her and then he is not a man at all, but a tall woman with a handsome, craggy face. And while I am confused and dizzy, the feeling of order goes on getting cleaner and cleaner, like things are connected way down, where I cannot see. I am confused and dizzy. I want to lie down.

"Ma'am? You look pale. Ma'am?"

Far away. His voice travels back from a moment ago. My tongue is dry and thick. The doctor leans up against the woman who is not a man and the woman wraps her arm around the doctor's shoulders and guides her away. They turn and walk up the road back to town. My skin stretches, the hard thing breaking through.

When I come to, I am furious. She led me out here to the desert, to them. The police. And not even the ones that could get things right, but the fuck–up ones that sit on their asses all day thinking about how the beer will smell when they pop that can and see what's on TV. I'm lying in a hospital room and that policeman's at home now, telling the story of some poor dead girl and making the story his, not hers. He's making that girl's death part of who he is so that what she was is not just gone but taken up and eaten and crapped out. All that's left is the sound of him grunting as he slowly eases down, like a man twice his age, into a large, soft chair. With cup holders.

I've got an IV in my arm, and I don't know what's dripping into me. But I've got to think things through before I make a move.

She's turned everything inside out. What does the doctor know?

I can't be tied down here. I can't lie around and explain myself to nurses or worse, the police. I must have passed out while we were talking. That one from last night will be back with questions about how I got here and why I passed out. He'll want answers, but he won't give me any in return.

I think I need more of what's dripping into me, but don't want to call the nurse. I have to get away and think. Can't do it here. There is a shadow across my door, the sound of washing up and then "You awake?" the nurse's voice is low and sugar sweet. I moan, keep my eyes shut. "I just need to take a few vitals then I'll leave you alone until morning. We can talk about how you're feeling later. Just rest now."

I don't even nod. She checks my pulse, my temperature, draws blood. I breathe long and shallow and do not flinch when the needle goes in. She switches off the light. When I don't hear her in the hall anymore, I'm up and out of there.

I grab a coat on the back of a chair in the nurse's station on the way out, and throw it over my gown. On the street, I catch the first bus I see. I'm in luck—we head out past the highway and go south, toward the lake. When the driver says we're as close as we're going to get, I get off and start walking.

Outside, the morning is blue-black. I hear the lake, wild and flat and sullen, like sour breath. I start walking as the stars blow out, one by one, and light slips in behind, welling up as if this morning were new.

I can only think of Doctor Renald, and how fast we are connected and why me to her and not Olivia, as if something important broke off and reattached where it doesn't belong. Something as deep in me as the tube that's still taped to me, stuck in my vein. Something only I could be fool enough to break.

No one's on the highway except a few trucks kicking up dust as they slam by. By six, the sun is coming up. I walk for over almost an hour until I find the turn-off and then follow the long road out to the shore. My car is still out by the lake, the only one in the lot. I have no keys, but it's open. When I reach below the seat for the spare key, I find a single sheet of paper with Olivia's jerky handwriting on it. She must have written it over and over to get it this nice because I can actually read it:

Mom,

Sorry I had to go. No, I want to cross that out. I want to throw this whole damn letter out. Because I'm not sorry. Not really. You know? Well, maybe you don't. That would be asking a lot I guess, given the circumstances. Even I can see that.

I've just got to get out. Consider it my graduation gift. Some kids get sent to Europe. I've got to make that for myself, right here. In my own weird way that no one gets, including me.

Do you know we don't fit in? Not just you, me too. You keep saying I'm pretty and young like that makes me okay. Kids at school think I'm pretty—pretty fucked up. They've been smelling it on me since grade school.

Maybe me going won't change anything. I just know I won't find out until I'm away from you. That's right. Now I've said it. Probably split your gut right open. If I did, I am a little sorry about that. I don't want to make you hurt. But I just can't get away from it.

See, I think there's things you can't give me. Or won't. Things maybe I should have had that would have made me more like other kids. I don't know what. I have to make them for myself now. It's up to me. And if I don't it's like I'll never get it ever. There's part of me that hates you for all of this, being screwed up and alone. But I think you're broken inside. In a way that can't be fixed. So maybe me turning out the way I am wasn't anything you could help. You're always waiting for things to fall apart. Always looking for it around the next bend. Well, now they have. Okay? So deal with it. We both have to deal now. I guess we'll find out what that means.

Livvy

I sit and read it through again. My girl. Here in my car. I don't know when. She could have dropped it in the day she left, and it blew beneath the seat. A real piece of her in my hand. Her words rip me. She knew they would, and she had the balls to say them anyway, to write it out on paper. Permanent. Like she'd never want to take it back or pretend it wasn't said. Good for her, I say. Good for her. I laugh, but not because it's funny.

When Olivia was five, she had a fright. I thought it would be one of those childhood passing fears. Like monsters under the bed or eating peas. I feel bad about it now.

There was going to be an eclipse. We walked up the long, dirt drive shaded by sycamores and eucalyptus until we could hear the murmur of neighbors on the road. We had to go right up to the end of the drive to see the sky. Olivia didn't want to go. But I took her hand, and we went. It was warm for late spring. Up away from the house at the road's edge, the bottle brush was in full bloom, and she sat on the ground, ripping the silky red spikes from the flower's cob.

The landlords, Jan and Tom, were outside too, and when they saw her tearing up their bush, they smiled and waved. Nice folks. I used to go to them when I ran out of milk, or they would give us avocados from their tree, just leave them in a bag on our front porch. He worked for the city, and she was a physical therapist. That's all I really knew about them. They were older, post-hippies, no kids, quiet, book-ish. Never raised the rent in fifteen years. Friendly but not interested in being friends. I liked them.

Up the street, that crazy red-head . . . what was his name, Lionel? Linus? He was prancing around a poster board on an easel with phases of an eclipse drawn out. He had a cardboard box mounted on a stand. A smart kid, but always stumbling, like there was so much going on in his head that he didn't know what his body was doing. As I watched, he tripped over the easel's leg and his mom, Bunny, had to move in quick to keep the whole set-up from falling apart. She was good at that, quick on her feet.

Lionel was the kind of boy who was curious about everything. Wanted to know how old I was and why Olivia didn't have a daddy and how many miles per gallon my old Datsun got. Then he would tell us everything he knew: the number of miles in a light year, why rabbits eat their own feces, that friction is the only reason why feathers and bowling balls don't fall at the same speed, and how babies have gills before they're born.

I bent down to see if I could get Olivia to leave the flowers alone. She asked if it was time to go back home, and before I could tell her no, Lionel was standing over us.

"Wanna know the best way to see an eclipse?" He fidgeted from one foot to the other.

"Thanks, Lionel. We're good here."

"You should come and see my set-up." He bent with his hands on his knees and talked to Olivia, "We can watch the eclipse through the camera I made. So we can see it without going blind." Then to me, "I read about it in Junior Science."

Olivia grabbed my hand, and pulled me back toward the house. Bunny was looking our way. In a second, she would come down to chat. I could handle Lionel but not her. She asked things like, "Gee, you have a lot of guts bringing up a kid alone. Do you have family in the area?" and, "She's so pretty, maybe she would like to have some of Becky's old party dresses?" Always trying to get me to sign up for selling cosmetics door-to-door. A pyramid scheme. Said she made enough to keep her kids in private school and then some.

"Shy, huh?" Lionel asked. He laughed as he reached into his pocket. "Hey, take these." He tried to hand her two index cards, but she wouldn't look at him. I think his wild red hair and freckles frightened her. She'd never seen him so close up.

I motioned him to back up, aiming to tell him he was too close, but he thought I was reaching and handed me the cards. One had a tiny hole in it.

"Hold them apart and let the sun shine through the hole. The eclipse will show on the other card. Like a camera, see? Like a pinhole camera. You know what that is?"

Now Bunny was coming our way. I knelt down, picked Olivia up, and walked away down the road. When I glanced back, Lionel waved and smiled happily. Behind him Bunny came, walking fast, brows knit, mouth hanging slack as she stared after me. She'd never caught on that I wasn't going to stop being rude.

Down the street we didn't know anyone. And there was more space, a sidewalk, a little breeze from the sea. When I showed Olivia the index cards she let go of me to reach with both hands.

"Look." I held one above the other so there was a white circle on the one below. She watched, then I let her hold them.

She stared down at that dot, crouched low, one hand on the upper card, the other splayed on the warm pavement. When it first began to change, she whispered, "It's happening, Mommy!" as if she knew as well as everyone what was going on. I watched over her shoulder as the white dot was eaten away.

Some kid we didn't know told her that we were watching the earth move, and she looked at him and then squinted up at me as if he was nuts. But she went back to watching until the light around us began to change, soft at first, like a dust cloth thrown over the sun.

The birds went quiet. Then someone said: "That's it! Look up! You won't see this again for maybe your whole life!"

She looked at me, and then beyond, straight up. I looked too. A giant black disc with fine ribbons of light fanned out from the edges like an underwater flower.

"The corona!" a voice said. The small word fell flat. The sight was fantastic. Beyond bounds.

I heard the sound of a small frightened creature. Not a whimper. It was fuller than that. The sound that goes with being caught and hanging limp. She was staring up, mouth open, face dead white. The light kept changing, brighter now. She was trembling. A bird sang. I covered her eyes and held her.

At first I thought she'd hurt her eyes, but that wasn't it. She could see just fine. She stayed inside afterwards, wouldn't leave the house for days, and didn't want to talk about it.

I read the letter again. The sea is flat and hot.

What did she mean things I can't give her? I gave her everything. But I know, too. I know what she means. I could go back over it all again. Try to rethink every decision, every lie, every time I turned away from what was closing in behind. But it would kill me, doing that. Not just because I can't go back and make a different choice. But because I would dare to think that would have made a difference. That somehow this world and my life in it can be managed.

What was it the doctor said? *It would be a shame to destroy that physical link. It's important, who we come from. It makes us who we are.*

My insides feel like they are banging together, loud and crazy like they are almost breaking but not. What I didn't give her wasn't mine to give. My body wouldn't hold her. It was not a place she could grow. Too small, too thin, too meager. But all the rest I gave her. Maybe I knew when I took her it wouldn't be enough but that only makes it worse. All this grew out of something I messed up from the start. Not just my body, me. I'm the dirt that things can't grow in.

I sit in the car and look at my face. The skin is fresh, pink where it's healing. The swelling from yesterday's surgery is almost gone. Soon, there will be no mark at all. *A new you.* If I could go back, undo, rebuild everything. But it's too late. My fingers on soft, new skin. Still numb. *I think you are broken up inside. In a way that can't be fixed.* Nothing she would want.

I grip hard, dig the nails in. The skin is soft. So soft I almost can't feel it.

I rake my fingers down.

All that loud, crazy almost-breaking gets quiet inside as my nails dig, long and slow, down my cheeks. The doctor tried to fix me, but nothing is worth fixing. Nothing is new. My insides sink. They keep dropping down where it gets quieter and more still. Down and down. I claw until my skin is sticky and slick.

I don't go home for days. My face is a wreck. I don't want the neighbors to see. I don't want the police stopping by to find out why I disappeared from the hospital.

One morning, I wake up beneath a desk in an insurance office where I clean. My mouth is dry. Tastes of old pickles. My face throbs.

I should be up and out of here. I can tell it's barely dawn. I hear footsteps in the hall. I wait for them to go. Shapes loom out of the dark. I don't like it here. The squat, rank office of a failing, family-run business. I think about the white, clean room at the clinic and what it would feel like to wake up there, a glass of water from the cooler, the smell of bleach and antiseptic. Maybe I would find more painkillers. I took the last one I had yesterday. After what I did, it's going to be a while before I can do without them. But it's not my night for the clinic, not yet.

I have to be careful. My hair's a mess. I tug my fingers through the tangles, pull myself out from beneath the desk and clear out. I bet by now the police have moved on to other things. Or maybe they never even came looking for me at all. They let a lot slide.

Traffic is light. Before I can think about it long enough to change my mind, I'm home. The house is quiet and still.

It's not just about the police and their questions. After finding that letter, after what I did to my face. Bruised, swollen welts where my nails tore the skin. I was scared to come back.

My own bathtub feels strange now. The clumsy shower-head on a handle, pathetic spray. Everything here is familiar but different. Like I've been away for a long time. Even so, there's my blue towel and my toothbrush and the silver butterfly clips I use to put my hair back. All the things I've been missing. I go to my closet and pick out fresh clothes. Everything is lined up like it's waiting. It feels dangerous, like picking through someone else's things. This strange world sits up against one that is familiar.

I put some stuff in my jacket pocket: a spoon, a shoe horn, and a piece of beach glass from the windowsill, things that will not be missed when the other me, the one who lives here, comes back.

I don't go in Olivia's room.

Just as I'm about to leave, there is a knock at the door.

"Asa? You home?"

Bunny.

"I haven't seen you around. I was worried. Please open the door."

When she sees me she buckles, hand on the door jam to balance herself. A flair for drama.

"My God! Asa! What happened?!"

"I'm okay, Bunny. I'm fine."

"Were you attacked? God, your face! Have you seen a doctor?"

I shake my head. Suddenly I feel weak. Standing face to face with Bunny is too much. I am afraid I will be sick.

"Let's sit down." She steps inside and directs me to the couch. "You look awful." We sit for a minute. She pats the back of my hand. I let her. I have been alone for days and days. Not spoken to anyone. I have forgotten words.

"You wait. I'll get my car. We're going to the ER and have you looked at."

I don't want to go. But I let Bunny run right over me like she's been wanting to for years. Her in my house, telling me what to do. It's kind of a relief. Not as bad as I thought. She takes me to the ER.

"You don't have to tell me what happened, if you don't want." Bunny sits forward, stretching her torso in its clingy orange blouse. Her hands wrap around one knee, her nails perfect splotches of mauve.

I nod.

"I mean, it's not necessary. But it might help. Did you call the police?"

I shake my head, glad she doesn't guess.

"It's not your fault. It's never your fault. But it's hard, isn't it? I mean having to relive it, having someone write it down."

She sounds like maybe she knows first hand about such things. Not about me, but about the story she is making up for me.

"They shouldn't get away with this. No one has the right. Do you understand?"

When the nurse puts us in a cubicle, we wait a long time while Bunny talks. Then the doctor comes, says I don't need stitches, and has the nurse squirt saline in the cuts and patch them up with some kind of oily salve and bandages. Turns out it looked a lot worse than it really was.

The doctor asks me what happened, and I tell him some lame story I can see he doesn't believe. He gives me a brochure with crisis-line numbers. Then he asks about my eyes. I'm surprised he noticed what's left from surgery. Pretty much all healed up by now.

When it's over, Bunny brings me home to her house, sits me down, and makes me a cup of herbal tea. It's an old-fashioned kitchen. Painted white built-in cabinets from the fifties and warped, green linoleum that's not much newer. What does her husband do? I thought he was lawyer. Somehow I thought she would have it more together.

Bunny sees me looking.

"I've almost got enough to redo it." She beams brightly. "Stan thinks it's an extravagance. But a new kitchen is one of the smartest investments you can make in a house. I tell him, but he doesn't listen. Why should he? He's hardly here enough to even notice."

"You've been saving?"

"Working my feet to the bone. I'm showing rentals now, but I'm going to get my real estate license. Trouble is, it's hard to make enough to keep up with the rising cost of remodels. I've almost had enough for over a year. But then, when I think I'm there, I call the contractor and he re-bids. It's always just a little bit more than what I've got."

"I thought you sold cosmetics."

"God, a lifetime ago! I'm still licensed, sell to a few friends, old clients, but it never took off the way I hoped."

"Seems like it would be nice, going to different neighborhoods, seeing how people live."

"Say the word, I can hook you up. But the real money's in houses." Bunny laughs and looks around her kitchen. "Maybe when the kids are out of college, I'll finally get this place the way I want it." She stirs her tea but doesn't take a sip. "Speaking of getting things the way you want, I heard you tell the doctor you had a lift. Good for you! I know it's been hard since Olivia . . ."

I set my cup down and stand. I don't want to talk about her. I thought we could avoid it, given the circumstances.

"Asa, please, sit."

And I do. Because it's dizzy up there.

"I didn't mean to upset you. I just wanted to say, if you are doing things for yourself, that's good. You should. You should just keep doing those things. Especially now."

Is that the answer? Do I just go on now the rest of my life doing things for myself? Is that how you get through?

"I had a lift a few years back. Funny, Stan had no problem paying for that. And the boob job. But then, well, guess we don't have to ask why there." She laughs sharply.

"Why?"

"Why what?"

"Why did you?"

"Why does any woman? Because we can. It's our elective choice these days. It seems a damn shame not to. We should make the most of what we have, you know? My poor mom lived her whole life despairing of her nose. She had great tits. Gorgeous tits. But she hated her nose. Back then, there was nothing she could do about it. Not without scandal."

"Was she shocked?"

"You mean about me? No. She's gone now. Has been for a long time. She died when I was fifteen. Cancer." Bunny grimaces. "It was gruesome in those days. I guess this was kind of my homage." Her hands flutter around her chest. "She was the most beautiful woman, even with that nose." Her eyes glow. "I miss her sometimes, even now."

I want to go back to the doctor, just to see her again, but I can't. Not after what I've done to my face. Things are piling up in my head. Things that should line up but don't. I think about the doctor holding my face in her hands and how everything felt calm inside, but remembering just makes everything worse.

One night at the clinic, I find her address on some blue-prints in her bottom desk drawer. At first, it seems like it's the right idea to go out there. I won't have to explain anything, just have a look around and see where she lives. No one has to know.

When I get there, though, I'm not sure. A white ranch-style house, sprawled against the hills. Behind her house is open space right on up to the ridge with a view all the way out to the coast. It's cooling off, and I wish I could dive with her into that aqua tiled pool, lay out damp on the sand-colored patio, and feel the evening breeze.

It would be a lot better if she wasn't with the man who's not a woman.

"Come on. Let's go for a swim," the doctor says. She knocks back the rest of her wine, kicks off her flip-flops, and steps into the pool.

"You go ahead," the other says.

"Come on. It's a beautiful evening." The doctor looks back. But the other does not move to follow, so she sits at the pool's edge.

He almost caught me at the edge of the patio, before the doctor came home. I didn't think she'd have a visitor, or I wouldn't have come. I was going to peek inside the back windows, but he came out, and I never got a chance. He's been soaking up the sun for hours. Drinking her wine. He even fed a scavenging coyote from her china.

"You don't have to be shy around me," the doctor says.

"I don't?" He's so coy.

"No. Come in."

"Can I be not shy enough to say no?" His voice is careful and controlled, neither low or high.

She pushes from the edge. Her body cuts the lit water like a knife. He watches her, perched gracefully on the end of the lounger, dressed in a softly draped wrap with gold and purple flowers on deep green. I settle in behind a knobby head of sage. The night is soft and the ground warm.

She comes up for air and props her arms up on the pool's edge.

"Look, I'm sorry I haven't been around much. Are you settling in okay?"

"The city's a shock to me—so many people, so much money thrown around. It's been a long time. I don't get out all that much, and when I do, I just want to come back. I love it here. Don't know how you make yourself leave every day."

I have stepped in something foul. A hairy turd left by some wild animal.

"Work. It's like that even when it's slow," the doctor says.

I try to wipe it off while I listen.

"Slow?" he says.

Why did she bring him here? I can tell why he came by the way he soaks up the luxury of her house. But why let him? Their voices drop. I edge in closer.

"A lot of no-shows. Appointments have slacked off."

"Maybe everyone's on summer vacations."

He pulls the wrap closer up around his shoulders.

"September's calendar should be filling up by now. People plan for when summer ends, before the holidays start."

She begins to swim with a strong, steady pace, up and down the pool. Once he glances in my direction but doesn't see me.

She has done ten laps when she stops and rests again on the pool's edge. She is breathing hard but not labored. She's stronger than she looks. One of those women who does things for herself. She gets out, towels off, her body shimmering in the pool's light.

"Do you want a drink?"

She walks into the house. He stands at the edge of the pool. Dips his toe in. Then wades to the first step. A breeze kicks up, and he lifts his face to it.

She comes back out with two full wineglasses and hands one to him. He sits at the edge of the pool. She scoots in next to him, close but not touching.

"I just need something that will get me back in the public eye."

"Like what?"

"Some success story. Something the magazines would jump on."

"Do some pro bono. Must be tons of people who need reconstruction from accidents or something."

"That's not exactly the market I'm looking to catch. It would be better to find someone people wouldn't feel sorry for, at least not in the same old way. Someone who wants big change, but elective. The outcome would have to be dazzling." He doesn't look at her. But I do.

Her voice is low. I have to strain to hear.

"I don't know, sometimes it all feels like a sinking ship. New technologies keep springing up, and I can't stay on top. Plus, it's been a hard year with the break-up. Clients can smell failure a mile away. I thought by now I'd be winding up, making the most of the years left before an early retirement. But if Clarissa gets half, I could be working until I'm ninety. I can't. I'd have to reinvent myself, heat up business. I just don't think I have it in me."

He puts his hand on her shoulder. They sit without speaking, sipping wine, feet in the pool, staring out at the hills and sky.

I steal away real slow. No one notices. Only a damn coyote. He darts from behind a bush and away. I almost shout out. A fast, dark shadow, he takes me by surprise.

I do not like that man at all. I make my way around the side of the house and back down toward the car. He acts like he understands, but he pretends a lot of things, this is just one more of them. I don't see how he can know how hard it is. She wants the chance to set something back the way it should be. She just wants to make something come out like it was supposed to. I get that. Out there on the warm ground with the soft glow of the pool and the open hills behind, it seems so simple. Not much to ask.

I let the car coast a little down the hill before starting it up. Then I head back to the clinic where I clean and clean until my knuckles are raw and my knees ache. I look again through her articles and think about her by the pool. How there's something that she needs, just one small thing she can make right. How she listens to him, even though he doesn't have the answer.

It bothers me. Enough that I need to see her. Face to face.

Bunny stops by early, before I can get out in the morning. She's wearing a pale pink velour running suit, but she's all made up and not out for a run. Her blonde hair is curled neatly at her shoulder. I tell her I don't have time to talk. She doesn't listen.

"I was thinking," she says, hand on the door frame, leaning in. I push past anyway and close the door behind. She follows, "I'm going to an information meeting next week for a course on how to create a high potential real estate career from the ground up. Want to come? It's free."

I look her over. Even in a jogging suit she looks nice and professional. That's when I remember the other business, door-to-door cosmetics, and I see my chance.

"You still have a connection with that cosmetic company?"

"You don't want to waste your time with that." Then she pauses, looks at me carefully, "I am still licensed. If you're really interested, you could be my trainee. I'd get part of your commission but that would save you making an initial outlay. It's expensive to get set up on your own."

"Do you get to pick where you sell?"

"We used to fight like dogs over territory, where the money is, where people will open their doors. But no one sells anymore. Now you'd pretty much have your pick of neighborhoods. I could tell you where the good ones used to be."

I'll bet she was a good fighter. Aggressive. Calculating. Not above a little backstabbing. Then at front doors with a great, big, cool-as-punch smile, and people would let her in, just like that. A clever, hungry dog in their living room. It's so funny, I laugh. She smiles, her eyes bright and sharp. We are beginning to understand each other.

Bunny made me late, but I am at the clinic before the doctor arrives. I don't like the way the receptionist keeps stealing looks at me, so I wait in the bathroom until I think she must be here. It's been weeks since what I did to my face, but people still look.

When I get back to her office, the doctor greets me. "I'm sorry to hear about what happened," she shakes her head.

I told the receptionist I 'had an accident' in an embarrassed way, so everyone would think it best not to ask. The doctor nods when I'm silent and then offers to have a look. I let her.

"Can you tell me more?" She says 'more' with a gentle inflection. When I don't say anything, she nods, sighs, then offers to have a look. I let her.

"The wounds are not so deep. They seem to be healing well. How long ago?"

"Almost a month."

"Did the ER prescribe anything to put on them?"

"Some cream. Antibiotics."

"You staying out of the sun?"

I nod. I know she is squeezing me in out of pity, and perhaps professional concern. But, still, she takes her time with me, and I appreciate that. There's so much I want to ask. Why she went out to the Salton Sea. If she knew I was there behind her. Who that man is at her house.

"I think you'll heal up fine." She smiles. She looks tired, her blue eyes a little milky.

I do not want to go, but she seems ready to let me. Maybe she's angry, disappointed about the scratches, but doesn't want to say so. It wouldn't sound professional.

"Is there more we could do?" I ask.

She goes back to her desk, eases gingerly into her chair. She seems old and frail in a way that frightens me.

"I've always hated the way I look," I add.

"Uh huh," she says and then straightens up, "You could come in for another consult. Just make an appointment. I'd be happy to talk to you about it."

I stand to leave. She doesn't look happy. She thinks I am just like everyone who comes through her door. Wanting to look beautiful, wanting to be young.

In the waiting room, there are two women who weren't there before. One young, one older. Both attractive. They look familiar. Rich. No one I would know. It's the mother and daughter, from the interview. I was thinking of Olivia when I read that article.

I go back out to the doctor's house on the hill. I'm looking up the long cobbled drive to her house. He is up there, soaking up the sun out back. I know it.

She said I would look better, like a younger me, when we were done. A young me. She thinks that's good, because she didn't know me then. And when she says it like it is good, I believe her. A different, young me. Her story of me on my face. Not so worthless after all.

Looking at that long, cobblestone drive with the pretty white house at the top, the pattern comes into focus. I see the thing I could never give to my daughter. My face, her hands. The doctor knows it, too. That long drive out to the lake was maybe just her way of telling me. The thing the doctor wants is not so different from what I need. Together we can make a story that is true.

Alexandra

I spend a whole week finishing up at Eleanor's house. I want to make this right, please myself at least. The furniture arrives, one piece at a time. Men with white gloves pull up in trucks and unload the club chairs, an Italian marble pedestal with the deco Egyptian urn, a modernist floor lamp with a black base and arrow-shaped paper shade, the mahogany and burl room divider table that folds out to a bar, a French vitrine bookcase with the original glass in the doors, the Decoux bronze Chardon.

All of it gets placed carefully where I say. I stack the bills on the kitchen counter. Eleanor looks them over, but I don't let her in the room.

I am just one more thing that confuses her. It will do her good to have her house back to herself.

One morning, there is a knock on the door and I hurry out, wondering what's arrived. I haven't checked the schedule.

It's Bunny. Still the same short, wiry Bunny, but different around the eyes. More haunted looking than I remember. More like Olivia.

"It's not a good time right now." I don't really want to ask her in. The last visit was so awkward.

She hands me my order in a glossy white paper bag with pink plastic handles.

"Next week?" She looks hopeful. She is wearing Eleanor's blue jacket.

Crazy. In all of L.A., it couldn't be. She looks nothing like Olivia in any other way, in height or build. The resemblance is so slight I think I must be imagining it, but I keep seeing Olivia looking out at me from this strange little woman.

I step inside the shadow of the door. "I'm going back home next week. I'm sorry."

"Oh." Bunny stands there, looking down, not turning to leave.

She looks up from the ground again, it takes a long time for her eyes to track up my body to my face. When she meets my gaze, it's like she's far away and too close, like she's looking at me through a window.

"You'll remember what we talked about? I mean you must have thought about it. You must know how things can be wrong, but put back together right."

She is doing that weird thing she did before. I feel pulled toward her while I resist. She starts to sway a little from side to side, and her face fills with the strangest smile. She looks at me with bright pity.

"You'll tell her, won't you? For both of us?"

I ease the door closed. Through the narrowing gap, I see her still standing there, just watching me.

When Eleanor comes home that night, she does not know the room is finished or that I plan to head out the next morning.

The sound of her calling through the house, "God! What reeks?!"

Emptied the trash. Cleaned the fridge. Can't get rid of that smell, though.

I'm sitting in the new room, the smell thickest there. I worry that it's worse because of something in the rug, but I can't seem to pin it down to that.

She flings open the door, "It's like something's rotting." She stops, takes the room in. "Oh, god, Alexandra. It's amazing!"

She has a drink in her hand and the ice picks up glimmers of pink from her linen blouse. She stands motionless and looks around, her face softening. A smile plumps her pale lips. "It really is very lovely. I had not expected. . . . I just didn't see how it was going to come together. But it does. It really makes the room seem right."

"I'm sorry about the smell. I looked everywhere. I can't figure it out." Aside from this damper on the moment, I feel flushed and a little shy about my own success. It is more than I expected, this bending of hers toward pleasure, completion, and gratitude.

She smiles, and waves her hand, "Whatever it is, it's got to wear off eventually."

"Good day at work?"

She laughs, eyes glowing, "Okay, maybe that's part of it. I've had some very happy clients. Plus, I got a call from my attorney. Clarissa finally signed the papers."

"That's great! You seem renewed."

"It was a huge amount, a little less than half. It's over, that's all."

"Business will pick up now that you can set your mind back to it. Maybe an interview with one of those happy clients?"

Her face darkens, "I don't think so. It's not the kind of work I want to advertise."

"Why not?"

She shrugs, "It's complicated." She looks around again. "The thing is, it's over. Clarissa is finally out of my life."

She springs up, now alert and playful, and sniffs the wall, hunched half over, down close to the baseboard. A breeze kicks up, and she turns toward the door. She walks outside, and I follow. She is right. It is stronger out here. I turn and head off behind the stone barbeque where a little path is worn between the grasses. My foot catches. A lump of wiry hair, coyote.

Eleanor hears my gag, and she comes over, bends down, hand over her nose and mouth.

"Damn neighbors. Poisoned. I knew it would happen. No chance they'll clean up the mess."

I fight the welling in my throat. "Why wouldn't he go off somewhere? Why would he come here?"

"He got too cocky around the smell of humans. Poor little bastard."

I feel even sicker now. "I fed him."

"You fed him?" Eleanor puts a cool hand on my shoulder.

"Sometimes. Gave him leftovers. He was so thin."

"You have a strange heart." Her words are gently clipped.

We shut the doors and sit inside. She stocks the bar in the new room, fixes us drinks, hands me one.

She sits next to me on the chaise, her thigh touching mine, and sets her hand on my knee. She looks up from her drink to scan my face and draws a long breath. Her voice calm and low, "If you have the surgery, you can stay."

"My god, El. I'm never going to be your patient. It's not going to happen. Even if I wanted plastic surgery, and I don't, I'd go to someone else because it wouldn't be right— we're friends."

"Not plastic surgery, the surgery. I know some fantastic gender reassignment surgeons."

"What?!" I stand, step back. She smiles sweetly.

"Come on, Alexandra. I have a feeling about this. It'll change your life. Free you. If you have the surgery, you can stay as long as you like. Live here, set up a business. Do what you want to do."

"You really are unbelievable! Jesus!"

She thinks she's offering me something, holding out salvation in her neat little hand. Her face is soft and pleading. "I just think things could be different for you."

"Yes. They could." I stop edging back and stand still. "But I don't want them to be. I don't want surgery, never have. It's simple. Trying to understand me any other way is just absurd."

I would like to stay on a while, let her lie all night in the shame of what she's said and pull away at dawn with strained farewells. But even this small token of apology, I suspect, is more than Eleanor can give.

If she hears me packing, she doesn't say anything. It's late, and she has already gone to bed when I close the front door behind me.

The next time I see Eleanor, it's months later, when everything out at the lake gets cool and quiet, just before the wildflowers bloom. It's midmorning when I get up, my head is thick, thoughts drugged with sleep. It does not really surprise me that Eleanor is sitting in my patio garden, tracing furrows in the sand with her fingers. But I'm not in the mood for guests. I let her wait a while, brew myself coffee, have a cup.

When at last I know she won't go away, I go outside and sit beside her.

"I've missed you, Alexandra." She smiles sadly. She looks small. It always surprises me how she starts out slight, hardly anything, and the longer we are together, the bigger she gets.

I cross my legs and take a sip of coffee.

"I would have called." She laughs without humor. "I did call. You didn't answer."

"I've been busy."

"Did they ever find that girl?"

"Olivia. Is that what you came here for?"

She looks at my coffee mug, folds her arms across her lap and huddles in a pathetically poised little way, "I came to see you." She sighs. "I really am sorry. I had no right."

"The thing that pisses me off?" I knew she would come, and I've been thinking a long time about what pisses me off, about Eleanor, about the city, about being back home. "At first I thought it was that you're always so completely off-base. Then I realized that you actually do see, or sense, little pieces of the truth. But you put them together to make up a picture that's all backwards." It feels good, getting the words out of my head. "It's unreal the way you mess it up. Uncanny, really. You have a knack."

"Sometimes I get it right. People say I do. They count on me."

"Clients, you mean. People who want to be changed."

"Not always."

She looks from the cacti and then skims blankly over the trailer. I follow her bewildered gaze and answer the question I suspect she wants to ask, "I enjoy the solitude."

"Just say, and I'll go."

That's the thing with Eleanor, when she's with me, she grows and all the hard feelings shrink. Until she makes a mess of everything again.

"Do you want coffee?"

"Please."

I fix it the way she likes, black with a little sugar, and go back out.

"I live here because it's on the edge of everything. It's quiet, cheap, and though it might not seem like it at first, it is beautiful here. Raw, in some way. Primal." I look at her plainly, "You keep coming back."

"Not because it's beautiful."

I stretch out in the metal garden chair, against the woven plastic backing, and wait for her to go on.

"You've got guts, I'll give you that. Living exactly as who you are. Most of us aren't that brave."

"You think so? What makes me braver than someone who decides to go through surgery? Or someone who lives as a man when they feel like they're a woman? What is courage when it comes to things like this?" I shouldn't egg her on by arguing. But I'd really like to know.

"That's not what I mean. I mean you know what's right for you, and you stick with it. It's admirable."

Admirable. Without the admirer, it's meaningless. Just like Eleanor to give a compliment that can't exist without her.

"Look, I became me little by little, one day after another, just like you or anyone. I make minor decisions every day, one by one. Gradually, they add up. Tomorrow will be a little different from today. Different decisions, different me. Nothing is fixed. Not really. At least, that's how it is for me."

She leans forward, cup cradled in her hands, elbows on her knees, "No. It's not the little decisions that make you. It's not." She sets the cup down. "I won't accept that. The little decisions don't make you, they wear you away. Decide to work late once. Then again. And poof!" Her fingers splay out, "A relationship falls apart. Take on a client who needs something you can't give, or shouldn't give. Because things are slow. And bam! Suddenly you're not sure if you're making things better or about to screw everything up."

"I don't really want to hear your confessions."

She looks at me as if across a wide open field. A hummingbird dips above our heads. A taut buzz. A flash of brilliant ruby, then gone.

"You want to go for a walk?" I ask. She looks surprised, but nods.

She changes into sneakers from the car and, as we pass back out through the patio gate, she asks me in a precise but casual way if I took her blue jacket.

"Yes, I did."

She hesitates, searching for a soft reproach, but either she doesn't find one or she has the sense to swallow it.

I lead her up the dunes. The heat is just beginning to gather at the base of the coming spike. It's still early. We get as far as the shacks out by the east bay without saying a thing. Just walking, me out front and Eleanor trailing behind.

The shacks were once little homes, before the lake swallowed them. They are an odd sight. Half submerged, their barnacled, salt-stained bones reflect darkly in the stagnant water. Rooms once lived in are now half sunk, windows without glass, doors ajar. Electrical conduits jut up from roofs and torn wires poke out at the air. Ordinary things. Taken up by sand crabs and brine.

She stands and looks but does not ask. After a moment, we move on, crossing a stretch of hardened earth cracked by sun and spring floods. Then over a small dune. Eleanor stops short. We are very near the place where Olivia camped. For one crazy moment, I think she senses the girl. But she has other ghosts to banish.

"I heard from Clarissa last week. She and her girlfriend broke up." She starts walking again, and I follow, almost at her side but one step behind.

"What did she want?"

"A shoulder to cry on."

"After what she put you through?"

"I couldn't turn her away. She looked good. She kind of glows when her life is wrecked."

"Eleanor. You didn't."

"Of course I did. I think she imagined this would heal us some way, after all that crap in the courts and the humiliation, she had the idea that maybe we'd spring back, stronger than before."

"You'd never."

"God, no. But I missed her body. I missed that place of complete abandon."

"And?"

"We'd forgotten each other. I thought the shape of her was written on me. But we'd forgotten." She shrugs and rolls her eyes.

I can tell there are things she does remember, though. Clarissa reminds her of when life felt on course, and they both believed Eleanor was the one who held it there.

She sighs. "It was a relief not knowing her. I was surprised, but it was a relief."

"How you remember her is still yours. I mean, that doesn't change." She doesn't answer, only gazes out at the lake. "So now you can move on?"

"I already had. Just didn't know." Her voice is flat and matter of fact. I wonder if this is what she'd come to tell me and, if so, why she is still so tight and miserable.

We go over another rise and come to a flat area that is more clear of brush and rocks than other places we've passed. Was this it? I try to picture the tent, the stove. There's no fire pit. An empty potato bag is caught in a weedy patch. Shards of a green bottle sparkle in the sun. The rocks might have been strewn.

"She was here, I think. This was where I met Olivia."

"Here?" Eleanor looks around, blinking.

"She had a canvas tent and a little fire."

"Why here?"

"She seemed okay. Like maybe she was going to figure it out."

"Maybe? My god, Alexandra! A young runaway and you think maybe she'll be okay? It's one thing for you to live out here, but a teenage girl in a tent?" She shakes her head and scowls. "Why did you bring me here?"

"Did I? Maybe I did. Makes me miss her."

Eleanor looks about her again, at the sterile dirt, the scrubby baked weeds, the flat, white water.

She sits down on the ground in her khaki slacks and hangs her head between her knees. After a moment, I go and put my hand on her shoulder. The bone is small and pointy. I remember the feel of her foot in my hand.

She does not lift her head. I crouch down next to her. Partly to comfort, partly because I am curious. Eleanor, letting go. She does not shake or cry.

She runs her hand up my arm, lightly, as if to thank me for being there. So I just wait. Then back down my arm again, this time slowly. She does not look up.

"Don't you ever just want to get out of the rut, do something unexpected?" I like seeing her where Olivia was; it somehow makes the ride of everything that came after seem less crazy. She looks a little destitute, begging me to see the edge she wavers on as daring. I like seeing her out here, tiny and disheveled on the dunes.

"Something unexpected, or something you want?"

She pulls away, looks at me icily. Then pretends not to be stung.

"I mean more than that." Her hand sweeps out, grabbing up the rolling dunes, the sky, and flat expanse of water all at once, tattering them with a flick of her clean fingers.

I think of the house again with the breeze blowing through and the heat of the dry earth wrapped in the sleepy smell of the sea. I miss the sound of cicadas opening up a night sky, how the pool's bright surface shook me from my dreams, the way the house stayed cool but never dim. I wonder what Eleanor did with the room. Did she really like it the way I fixed it up? Or did she clear it out, fill it with French antiques?

Looking in her cold blue eyes, I am frightened. Twenty years ago, I would have let the whole of her deluge me. The untouched quiet of casual, elegant living, the blue tile beneath water, jacaranda filtered light. I might have thought myself lucky. Rescued. Reborn. She leans in close, smells of cooled, milky tea. Soft. Sweet. Her lips touch mine. Not Eleanor's at all, but some girl's. I taste the salt of her skin, the wet of her mouth.

She goes very still. Only the murmur of the highway. I don't pull away. I don't reciprocate. I just let her find her own way, stumbling over risk and uncertainty.

She stirs and stands. Pulling her jacket down to the bone of her hip, brushing dirt into her slacks, smoothing hairs that have not come loose; she does not look at me. She takes a few steps and then stops.

"Are you sure you have my jacket?"

"I took it, yes."

"It can't possibly fit you."

"No. It doesn't."

She nods and turns away.

As I watch her go, I think how it must have been the morning Olivia left. For a moment, I imagine I see the girl out in front, bag slung over her shoulder, striding over the rough ground. She is strong and young, a violet heat. Then, the image of her is gone. And so is Eleanor. I am alone on the dune, thinking of Olivia, of Bunny, of Eleanor. Of the blue jacket. The dunes roll out toward the wide, flat mirror of the lake.

Sometimes now when I go out past the shacks to the dunes, I sit till sunset when a breeze kicks up and tears across the lake, making its steely surface writhe. I can't picture Eleanor here anymore. When I think of her, she is at home alone. Her eyes closed. Her face sweet. A drink collecting beads of sweat. I do not know if this is how she is. Maybe only what I want for her.

The light on the desert hills is dusky purple and cool. I don't look for the spot where Olivia camped. Too many naked little clearings. I don't try to remember.

I think I won't go back to the city ever. Then, months later, when the days start heating up again, I do. I rent a car and drive out to L.A. At first, I head back to the old neighborhood, just to see. I pull off at Fairfax and cross Wilshire. I think about stopping but don't. Traffic to a new mall is backing things up and making it impossible to park. Not today. Instead, I head south across the city to where Olivia said she lived. It's a small neighborhood. I ask around. People know about her and her mother. I find the mailbox at the bottom of a hill, then a long overgrown driveway. I park the car, walk down.

The place is a small, cedar-shingled bungalow tucked back inside a grove of tall oaks. There's a low front porch with a broken swing. I look through the glass-paned door and see a bare-floored living room. Nothing but a couch, a low coffee table, and a couple of wooden chairs. I knock. No one comes, so I try the knob.

The place is empty. No knickknacks, no clutter. The fridge is unplugged. I walk through.

In the one bedroom, a threadbare towel hangs over a hook on the wall but there are no sheets on the bed. In the bathroom, a stained-glass window throws dappled blue on a dingy stone floor. The water from the tap is brown.

A woman's voice calls from the front of the house, "Hello?" Cheery, confident, welcoming. "I saw your car up by the road. Sorry I'm late. Have you seen the house?"

"No," I step into the hallway and see her standing in the living room. She is a middle-aged woman, nattily dressed, hair in a tight coif. She looks confused but continues to smile brightly.

"I'm Bunny." Bunny? Not my Bunny.

"I show the house when the owners are out of town." She steps toward me and extends her hand.

"It's for sale?"

"For rent. I thought we had an appointment." She glances at her watch. "If it's not with you, then what are you doing here?"

"I'm looking for Olivia's mother."

Her eyes widen and then narrow. "Olivia? Have you seen her?"

"No. Not for a long time. But I'm trying to find her mother."

"Asa's been gone a while." She examines me carefully, "You don't know, do you?" When I don't respond, Bunny nods. "She was in a bad way after Olivia left. Had a real hard time of it."

"What happened to her? Did she just clear out? Is she under care?"

Her eyes widen. "Oh, she's under care. Lock and key. But that's not what you mean, is it?"

She pats my arm and nods, "You a friend?"

"Not really."

"Not a reporter are you? Nosing around?"

"I knew Olivia."

She looks at me carefully then nods again and says, "Wait here. I'm just going to pop back home, I live a few doors up."

I hear her walk up the drive. Everything is quiet for a while. When she comes back, I am sitting in the small room at the back of the house. There is a single, stripped bed and a low bureau. Nothing in the closet.

"Here." She hands me a stack of newspapers and magazines.

I stare at her dumbly.

"I'm in the grey Cape Cod, second on the right up the hill. Drop them by when you're done." She looks me up and down. "Lock up when you go, okay?"

I flip to the dog-eared page in the magazine *L.A. Living* and read the article called "Therapy Out, Plastic Surgery In? The New Path to Inner Peace."

It's an interview at the state prison in Bismark, North Dakota. Asa Hornby, a.k.a. Bunny, looking eerily like Olivia, smiles out from the page. She's dressed in light blue smock-like shirt and jeans. Frightening now, to think of her across from me in Eleanor's living room. At the bottom of the page is the Asa I knew, drab and hunted-looking.

Sergeant Al Barnett: "She just walked right in and gave herself up. Eighteen years later. It floored me. I'm not condoning what she's done, any of it. But to hand yourself in after all this time? That takes guts."

Prison Officer Natalie Shrenker: "She's a model prisoner. Studying for her GED and planning to apply to community college. I try not to pass judgment. Never gave us one day of trouble. That's all I know."

Asa Hornby: "I know I've done a lot of wrong, hurt a lot of people, and I regret that. I do. But, even if I never get forgiveness, I found something, the strength to come clean, start over maybe. It's not everything, but it's a start, some peace for once, my own kind of peace."

Dr. Eleanor Renald: "It is a radical example of how physical change can be a catalyst to profound emotional catharsis. She needed to find her way back to her daughter. The work we did began that process. It took a great deal of emotional integrity for Asa to turn herself in. That says something, I think. I do hope, for Asa's sake, that the circle is completed. That, one day, she and Olivia are reunited."

Reporter: "Are you saying surgery is a kind of therapy? Are you really condoning this as a method for emotional relief?"

Dr. Eleanor Renald: "I would never do this unless I was working closely with the client's psychiatrist. It's intensely cutting edge, so to speak. No doubt inappropriate in a majority of cases. But if someone feels that is the only way forward for them, perhaps it is not so crazy to consider the idea."

Dr. Janice Thompson, Asa's psychiatrist, declined to comment.

I read all day, sitting on the low bed. There was a bit of a scandal about Eleanor's comments, but with no one bringing a suit against her, the publicity only boosted her reputation. The look took off. In one article there are photos of five different women who look like they could be Olivia's sisters. By the time I got to the bottom of the pile, articles reference talk shows, a forthcoming book, and a new clinic in Beverly Hills. I read until it's dark, and I can't see the page. I lie back and close my eyes to rest for a few minutes before the long trip home.